Nowhere Girl

Nowhere Girl

A. J. PAQUETTE

WALKER & COMPANY

First published in the United States of America in September 2011
by Walker Publishing Company, Inc., a division of Bloomsbury Publishing, Inc.
www.bloomsburykids.com

For information about permission to reproduce selections from this book, write to Permissions, Walker BFYR, 175 Fifth Avenue, New York, New York 10010

Library of Congress Cataloging-in-Publication Data
Paquette, Ammi-Joan.
Nowhere girl / A. J. Paquette.
p.   cm.
Summary: Fair-skinned and blond-haired, thirteen-year-old Luchi was born in a Thai prison where her American mother was being held and she has never had any other home, but when her mother dies Luchi sets out into the world to search for the family and home she has always dreamed of.
ISBN 978-0-8027-2297-3
[1. Identity—Fiction.   2. Voyages and travels—Fiction.   3. Americans—Thailand—Fiction.   4. Fathers—Fiction.   5. Families—Fiction.]   I. Title.
PZ7.P2119No 2011   [Fic]—dc22   2010049591

Book design by Nicole Gastonguay
Typeset by Westchester Book Composition
Printed in the U.S.A. by Quad/Graphics, Fairfield, Pennsylvania
2 4 6 8 10 9 7 5 3 1

All papers used by Bloomsbury Publishing, Inc., are natural, recyclable products made from wood grown in well-managed forests. The manufacturing processes conform to the environmental regulations of the country of origin.

For my mother

Nowhere Girl

For the first time in days, I hear voices. I'm curled over on myself, pressed into my cramped hiding spot, clinging to the dark like it's a life jacket.

The voices move closer.

They'll pass by, like they have before. They'll go somewhere else. They have to.

But they don't.

Laughter roars just above me, and through a chink in the tarp I see dirty gray running shoes move closer. I push myself tighter into a ball. They don't know I'm here; maybe they won't see me. Then the cover is ripped away and everything moves very fast: a roar of frigid air, a blinding wash of light, men's voices raised in shock and alarm.

I've been discovered.

Just as quickly, the tarp falls back on top of me. I am alone with my terror. The voices mutter to each other, growing louder and harder and fiercer.

They were caught off guard, but they'll soon decide what to do. They'll rip away the cover for good this time—and then what?

My heart is pounding pounding pounding in my chest, so loud I can hardly hear the splash of waves outside. Everything around me blurs. I need something familiar, something I know. The bars! Where are they? The bars will protect me. If only I could find them . . .

But of course I can't. My prison bars are gone, far away with Mama and all the rest of my past.

It's no fairy tale, this life of mine. It's no dream. I'm just an ordinary girl born into a web of secrets, trying to unravel it strand by strand. Trying, somehow, to find my way out.

It's been a long road to bring me here, to this pallet, seconds away from discovery and capture. And has it been worth it?

I close my eyes and I am there, living those memories like it's the first time.

PART I

Departure

1

There's a tree that grows just outside the prison compound—a twisted old thing, curled into itself, bark into leaf into hard-packed ground. A tree like that's got character, I think to myself, looking out at it through my bars. On nights like this I can see it clearly, all craggy and hunched over, backlit by the fat moon. That tree probably started out smooth and straight and proud, one day so long ago. But then something went wrong, something inside the tree or maybe outside got it growing the wrong way. And the tree started to bend and twist, to turn over into itself. Maybe becoming an inside-out stump was the only way it could survive.

Surviving. Is that what I'm doing?

I look around the tiny cell where I've lived my whole life. In her bunk, Bibi lies flat on her back, snoring loudly. Jeanne has her hands bunched in tight fists, wary even in sleep. My cot is on the floor, next to Mama's bunk. Her bunk that is still empty, almost three months later.

Why am I still here? Every day Chief Warden Kanya says,

"Tomorrow, I am calling the American embassy. Shameful, a young girl wasting away in a place like this!" And every day I beg her to wait just one more. Give me a little more time, I tell her. I need to prepare myself to face the world. Figure out what I'm going to do once I get out there.

And what I don't say is that truthfully, I do not want her to call the embassy at all. If Mama taught me nothing else, she taught me this: Keep your head low. Stay out of sight. Do not get involved with the outside world. Of course, I can't say any of this to Chief Warden Kanya. There is so much that she does not know. There is so much that *I* do not know.

But the days pass, and I know I will need to act soon.

My eyes flick back to the window. The tree looks like a lumpy, black paper cutout against the hot white moon. And for some reason I keep wondering: if someone had been there with water and care, if someone had come to fight off the pests, would that tree have grown up clean and straight?

And if so, would it have been better off? Or do all those gnarls show the tree's strength? Are they evidence of a life wasted or a life lived full?

I decide that I love that tree more than anything else in the world.

And with that I make up my mind: I've had enough of waiting. Chief Warden has bent the rules for me as long as she can. If I don't act soon, she will call the embassy despite my protests. Mama's gone, but she's left me instructions. Now I need to start growing on my own.

It's time for me to leave Khon Mueang Women's Prison.

2

Here's what I know about myself. My name is Luchi Ann, and that's all the name I need for everyday. I didn't know any more of my name until three years ago, when I was ten, and Mama made me promise never to tell it to a soul.

It's not the only thing she made me promise.

Here's what I know about my mama. Her name was Helena and once upon a time she was tall and blond and beautiful. I know this because of the wooden tea box that holds all my most important things. Chief Warden Kanya gave me the box after Mama's passing. It stays in the office for safekeeping, and every few days I like to go in there and pull everything out, look over each item carefully. In that box is the photograph—the one showing Mama before. There's also a Thai paper that tells how I was born, right here in the back exercise yard of Khon Mueang Women's Prison, up north of Chiang Mai. And there's Mama's passport and a bunch of dollars, real American dollars that I never get tired of touching. The paper feels soft but strong, like a whispered promise you know will be kept.

A promise is something I understand. It's the glue that holds together my world. My mama always said her secrets were her backbone, what made her strong.

"We are behind bars, but we are alive," I remember her telling me, back when I was too young to wonder what her words really meant. "Here we are safe, Luchi, remember that. No one knows who we are, so we can't be hurt. Promise me you'll never do anything to change that."

I linked my pinkie finger with hers and gave my solemn promise; then I leaned into her arms and we held each other until the bell clanged for lights out. We made a strong rope, Mama and me and our secrets.

But then everything changed.

I don't like to think back to her last few weeks, when the fever came. Mama had been the whirlwind in our cell, the joker, always making us laugh. How many hours we spent with Bibi, our cellmate, rolling across the floor laughing at her crazy stories! She could even get a chuckle out of our other cellmate, Jeanne, on some days. I think we all knew Mama laughed so much to stop us from seeing the tears she kept hidden inside, but we played along. Mama was like that. People would fall all over themselves to do what she wanted.

This fever was different than anything we'd seen before, though. With the heat came pain, then blood, and one day when I looked close, my mother was a black-and-white sketch of herself. The tears were gone, but so was the smile, and so was the spark, and so was everything that made up the real *her*. That last day, she reached one twig arm toward me as I sat cross-legged on her bed, where I had been since the start of her sickness. She grabbed my finger with her whole hand, tried to hold on and couldn't, so I held on to her instead.

"Luchi," she rasped, and it was all I could do to hear, so I leaned in closer. "I'm not long for this world. You'll have to make your way out of here. Have to be strong, do what I could never do. You'll have to go . . . home."

"Home?" I looked around the prison cell that was my whole world and wondered what she could possibly mean.

"I didn't tell you enough about my past. I thought there would be time. I thought—" She coughed, a spasm wrinkling up and down her body. "I thought we would leave here together . . . someday. When it was safe."

"We will, Mama," I said, squeezing her hand tighter. "Tomorrow you'll feel better. Sleep now." But tomorrow would be no better. Even I could see that.

"All those promises, all those things I told you." Mama's eyes were bright now, her cheeks scarlet. "Remember them . . . don't . . . do them . . . you've got to remember that, will you? All those promises, all those secrets . . . all right? Will you? Won't you?"

I looked up at Bibi, confused. What was Mama trying to tell me?

Bibi just shook her head. "*Lap dee dee na ja,*" she

whispered, stroking Mama's short hair. "Sleep is the best thing for her now."

I nodded. Bibi was right. Mama's eyes drifted shut, and I loosened her hand from mine and set it down carefully at her side.

Eight hours later she was gone, without ever waking up. Without ever explaining to me what she had been trying so hard to say.

Chief Warden came to me the next day, asking about relatives and officials and moving on, but I just cried and begged for more time. How could I leave? Sure, I had been out in the world before—to the courtyard nearly every day, and into Chiang Mai with the guards on certain occasions. Once I spent five days with my favorite guard, Isra, at her family home. They treated me like a princess, and even now, that memory is rich and sweet. But that world was never my own. Now, the only person I belonged to was gone. Was I also supposed to leave the only place I had ever lived?

And what about the unnamed danger that lurked in the outside world? I'd never gotten Mama to tell me *what* it was we were afraid of. How could I hide properly if I didn't know what I needed to stay hidden from?

Go home, Mama told me, but she left me nothing of that place. To me, at least, it did not exist.

3

And now I sit on a straight-backed wooden chair in Chief Warden Kanya's office, watching her watch me. Her eyes are like cups of tea, big and dark and wet.

"What people do you have on the outside?" she asks, pulling up the question like a familiar tune. "Tell me about your mam's family."

We have had this conversation almost every day for the last three months. And now that I have told her I'm leaving, she thinks I will finally be glad to accept her help. But I only shake my head and lower my gaze to the desk. I must leave this place and face whatever dangers I might find on the outside. I know this. But I will not abandon my promises so easily.

"You must have relatives, yes? I can call them and make arrangements. They could come and meet you."

I cannot tell her these things she wants to know. What Chief Warden doesn't understand is that I am not just being stubborn. How can I tell her what I don't even know myself? My silence was Mama's last wish, but my ignorance was carefully formed over my whole lifetime. And this is the full truth I cannot reveal: I know nothing of my past, nothing beyond my own name, and that I am sworn never to tell another soul.

Yet I know Chief Warden will not give up. She runs a prison; she has enough patience for many lifetimes.

Sure enough, she pulls out her favorite line. The one that always gets me talking. "I still do not know why I haven't called the embassy. Such negligence I could be charged with! A minor, an American child at that . . . I should call them right now." Her hand hovers in the direction of the phone, then slumps back to the desk.

She won't call them. Every day that she has waited; it would look worse for her to finally do so. I think by now it is too late. Three months later? What would she even tell them? But underneath her prickly surface, I know the chief warden is worried for me. She will not let me leave her care without knowing that I will be safe. And so I rip a tiny hole in my silence and pass out some of the truth she so desperately wants to hear.

I have had time to prepare for my departure, and I now have a starting point: an old sheet of paper found in Mama's things, a paper listing names and addresses and telephone numbers of people in Bangkok. It isn't much, and all the folds and wrinkles show my treasure's age. How reliable can this information be, after all this time? Yet I have nothing else. This is my only link to my past.

It is a start, and that is enough for me.

All of this is more than Chief Warden needs to know. She does not need to see the very thin bridge I am stepping out upon. I only need to reassure her, and then be on my way.

"Here," I tell her, waving the paper just out of reach. "Mama has many friends in Bangkok. She has written them all down. Once I get there, these people will know what to do. They will help me."

Chief Warden knows how Mama was, how close she kept her past, so she cannot have expected me to hand her a phone number now, an easy call to make everything okay. But she sighs. Maybe she hoped I would be different.

"Very well," she says now, and I hear resignation in her tone. "I have called my nephew, Kiet. He is driving to Bangkok today and can take you with him. Once you are there, you can find these friends?"

I nod, not for the friends but for the nephew, a minor celebrity in our world and a long-ago friend of my childhood. He comes to visit on holidays, and he usually brings a crate of papayas or rambutan for his aunt and the other guards. A few choice pieces of fruit always end up on my cot. I do not know him well anymore, but I know I will be safe driving to Bangkok with him. I look up at Chief Warden and give her a small smile.

Her eyes droop and I know she wishes there was more she could do. But how can she? Mama was strong in life, and she is strong in death. She has set out the path that I must follow.

Chief Warden starts to talk. "I still remember the day your mam came through those doors. We don't get many foreign transfers—our facility is usually considered too small and too far north to bother with. But crowding was extra bad that year and we had the space, so Bangkok sent us a shipment. Six or eight prisoners, and all of them terrified of what this relocation would mean for their futures." She sighs. "But your mam was different. It was almost like she wanted to be here, in this up-country prison on the far side of nowhere. You would have thought her greatest wish was simply to be forgotten."

I swallow, because those words have the taste of the familiar.

"She looked at this prison like she was stepping into a dream, and when I asked her about the American embassy, about calling family, about sending out letters, it was always the same."

I say the words in my mind along with Chief Warden. Lord knows I've heard them enough times over the years: "'No, thank you. There is no one out there for me. I will remain where I am until my time has been served.'"

She shakes her head. "Then after a few months we found out that you were on the way, and of course we all thought that would change her. That perhaps a man— your father—might come for you, might bring your mam to her senses. But no." Chief Warden studies me, like she's trying to read in my face the answers she's looking for. She sighs. "What am I saying? Of course you know your own mother's story! You must have heard this many times before."

I fix my eyes on the ground. I have to keep them there because looking down helps me set my mouth in a straight line. If not, I might open my mouth and say what I'm really thinking, which is: No! I don't know anything about my mother's past. She hid from me, hid from all of us. I don't know her stories and I don't know her life.

My *father*? I choke down a bitter laugh. Mama's only responses to my questions on that subject were downward spirals of depression that lasted longer and longer, until I finally gave up asking. And now she has taken her fear—and her secrets—to the grave.

Or has she? With a quickening heartbeat I look down at the sheet of paper clenched in my hands. Maybe these scribbled notes are a map Mama has left me to figure out my future. Maybe, from these words, I can begin to understand what she used her last breath to try to say.

Chief Warden struggles heavily to her feet. "You should go back to the cell now and prepare your things. Kiet will be here by noon."

I stand and lift my eyes to meet hers. There's a strange lightness in my chest. Chief Warden's story of my mother's arrival is not much on its own, but now I wonder: what other secrets might be out there, waiting to be discovered? For the first time since making my decision, I look toward the door and consider whether the outside might not only be a place to fear—but maybe, also, a place to search for answers.

Somewhere out there is my mother's story, the whole story. And I must find it.

The chief warden has no more things to tell me. She lowers her head and whispers, "*Luuk*." Daughter. She has called me this only once before, and it surprised me back then, too.

I was a skinny little runt, and I used to think the bars of our cell were some sort of pen to slide out of, a joke between friends. I could turn sideways and slip through them like a pit from a mangosteen, and when I did I was proud enough to dance, shrieking, up and down the corridor.

The guards mostly just laughed, letting me rattle around and make play-corners for myself. Isra would hold me on her lap sometimes and let me listen to her radio while I made chains out of the paper clips on her desk. In those times the world was one giant game, created for my enjoyment.

But the chief warden was made of sterner stuff. A job was a job and a jail was a jail—so she said, and often. Isra and the others could hear her footsteps coming down the hall and would trundle me back into the cell before she got there. One time, Isra was in such a hurry she forgot to take back the pocket radio she'd been letting me use. I listened for hours before she returned to get it.

After a few more years, I started learning about cells. Not about prison, exactly—that came later. But I learned the bars weren't there for my fun after all. They were like teeth, long and thin and sharp, that stayed there all day and night, grim and menacing. I wasn't sure they meant me harm, but I began to keep my distance.

And then one night my worst fears came true.

It was late, and I hadn't been able to sleep. Some months had passed since I'd last climbed through the bars. But Isra had left her radio out and I could see it on the guards' desk, calling to me. Mama and the others were sound asleep and the cell was dark. Maybe the teeth were sleeping, too, and then how could they bite me?

I pushed through. My leg slipped smooth and then my shoulder and half my body. My head came next and I had to turn it to the side—how did those bars get so close together? I pushed hard, and then I knew I'd done wrong. I thought the teeth were sleeping but they weren't, they were awake, just lying quiet in the dark and now they had me tight and they wouldn't let me go.

I was stuck. No amount of moving could get me in or out.

I didn't dare make any noise, not even a whimper. I wasn't eaten yet, but the second I made a sound I knew it would all be over. I thought of Mama, just out of my reach. If only I could stretch a little farther, quietly shake her awake—

But no. Mama, too, was afraid of the bars. I'd seen her stare at them, seen the fear in her eyes when she thought I wasn't looking. She couldn't save me from the jaws of this cage. And so I brought my hands up to the bars in front of me and held still, so very still.

Time passed like this; I stayed frozen while the moon moved from one side of the cell window to the other.

And then feet clattered in the hall: Chief Warden Kanya was making her rounds. She marched through and her flashlight glanced over me, trapped as I was. She startled, nearly dropping the light, but then she squatted down and shone her beam full on me and I'd never before seen her look so soft.

She called me *luuk*, little daughter, and she pushed and poked and got me back through the way I'd come. She kept those teeth away. And then she looked at me and she put one hand on the side of my face, where the skin felt hot and mushy, like bruised fruit.

I didn't understand her look then. But I think I do now. I think she was just a warden doing her rounds and checking up on things and then she comes upon this child stuck in the bars. Stuck between inside and outside, not able to move, not really a part of either. Trapped in between two worlds.

I think maybe that night she saw me real for the first time.

The next day she tried to talk Mama into letting me leave. "Surely you have family in your country who can take her. She is a growing girl, and she needs to live in the real world. Not in this—this place!" Chief Warden was fierce as a tiger, glowering right into Mama's face.

But Mama never flinched. She got that look she had sometimes, that empty look like a mask with no eyes behind it. "We have no one," she said. "No one who can help."

And I knew Mama would fight for me, take on the world to protect me from the danger that lived on the outside.

The chief warden never brought it up to her again. And when Mama died and I said I wanted to stay on just a little longer, she pressed her lips together and wrote out a schedule of duties I could perform around the prison in exchange for my room and board. For these last months I've slept nights in my cell with Bibi and Jeanne, while the chief warden has looked the other way and left me alone with my grief.

"*Luuk*," Chief Warden Kanya says again. She pulls me out of my remembering and I am back in her office. Back in this world where I am grown, where I am alone, where everything is different. Why can't I be different, too? I could be a strong, confident girl. I could have no dark shadows in my life, no unknown secrets forcing me to stay hidden. What would I do, if I were that other me?

It's no use.

Inside, I'm still that scared little girl, trapped between my fear and my promises and just wishing my mama would wake up and save me, help me, tell me what to do.

For a second a wave of grief crests inside me, and I know if I let myself sink into it I will drown, truly drown in my sorrow. I will slip under the surface and be swallowed whole. And then I will never leave this place.

But there is a part of me that has to leave.

And so I push down inside me and squeeze with all my might. Mama's gone. I am alone. But I am still alive.

Holding my tea box in trembling hands, I turn away from Chief Warden Kanya, who is now crying real tears that are making my eyes more blurry than they should be. The plastic watch on my wrist tells me there are just a few hours to go, and a whole world to learn to live without. I move away quickly and hurry out of her office.

My old life is gone forever.

4

This is my last walk down the hall, the long hall from Chief Warden's office and up the stairs to our cell block. The prison feels crooked around me, seeing it as I am for the last time. It's like I'm a cut-out paper girl stuck back on top of the page where I started, but I don't fit anymore. The edges are all wrong.

Voices call to me from the cells I pass. Women reach out their hands, some women I know well and others I don't. They croon and coo and brush their fingers over me, this little bit of prison that is heading out to the world. They want to touch this bird that is about to fly free, like maybe some bit of their touch, too, will go out there and see the world. Feel the world. So some part of them can live again.

But I am no bird and I have no wings. I've only got a big empty spot inside me where once I had a mother, once I had a home, and now there's nothing.

Bibi and Jeanne are out on work duty, and I am alone when I enter the cell. I drop onto Mama's bunk, reach underneath, and pull out the small clay jar that holds her ashes. It is dull and unpainted, and if I stretched my fingers wide around it the tips would almost touch. But I can't seem to open my hands. They are stiff and tight and cold, and through their shaking I can hear the rattle of the little clay lid.

Even after all these weeks I can hardly bear to hold this jar. How can such a small container be all that is left of my mama? What about everything that made her alive . . . where did all that go? What about the pale yellow hair that spread like a spiky fan on her pillow every night? What about her big wide dance steps as she spun me round and round the cell? And what about her smile, what about her laugh, what about her jump and her spark and the way she *was* that would never, never fit in a secondhand clay jar in a forgotten jail cell somewhere in northern Thailand? How could one urn ever hold her?

Standing, I pull the sheet from the bed, bunch the faded cloth, and lift it to my face. Despite many washings, there are still traces of her. For long seconds I just stand there, filling my lungs with the familiar, comforting smell. Then I clench my hands and set my jaw. I rip the sheet all the way down the middle, a long, hollow sound that is like the breaking of my heart. I rip until all the feeling inside me is consumed in this one motion, over and over and over. Finally I'm left with a pile of ragged yellowish strips.

I pick up the first strip and begin to wind it around the urn. One wrap for safekeeping. One for warmth. One for guidance. I wrap and I twist until the urn is lost in folds of faded bedding.

Now, if I don't look too closely, this rough-shaped ball might be something else completely. It might not be my mama at all.

There is a groan from the door behind me, and I turn to see Bibi, her glassy eyes on the bundle in my hands. I set it on the bed and fall into her arms.

As far back as I can remember it's been us four in the cell: Bibi from the northern province of Phayao; Jeanne from the exotic, faraway city of Paris; Mama and me from America. Bibi was my playmate, a wide warm woman with a ready smile and a heart that hugged the world. I never knew what brought her inside, but whatever it was, I don't believe it. My Bibi taught me games and poems, and told me long stories in Thai that first lulled me to sleep, then awakened me on the inside, then sent my imagination off places I never knew existed. Safe inside my walls, I traveled the world.

Jeanne was thin and sharp as a switchblade, but she had the mind of a scientist. She could be cold, and usually was, but she took it upon herself to grow my brain. Sums and equations, formulas and calculations . . . It was like she was shucking off on me all the knowledge that had gotten stuck in her head over the course of her life.

Everyone knew what Jeanne was inside for, though apparently no one thought I was old enough to hear it. It had to do with knives and explosives, but that's as much as

I could get out of anybody. Anyway, it didn't matter, not really. That's the thing about life on the inside: whatever you were before matters less and less as time goes on. Inmates craft their own worlds, build empires and elect rulers and live their lives, as though everything that happened before never was at all.

Of course, most people have *had* a before. I've always felt like a monkey in the middle—a saying I once read in a book and never forgot because it fit me so well: American but not American, Thai but not really Thai. Where do I belong, with my pale skin, my corn-silk hair, my stone-gray eyes? How can I call any country my own?

Now Bibi holds me tight and strokes my hair, like she has ever since I can remember. I'm not sure whether my leaving will be harder on me or on her, but we both know it has to be.

I dry my eyes and offer her a wan smile.

"You are ready," she says, and I nod, squeezing her hands hard. Moving back toward the bed, I set down my tea box and pick up the bundle that holds the urn. I loosen and stretch part of the wrapping, yank the knot tight, and pull it over my shoulder like a carry-bag. Then I glance under the bunk at my belongings.

Skirts and pants and T-shirts. Sarongs. A doll I twisted out of green palm leaves. The school supplies of my childhood: the Merriam-Webster dictionary that I read and recited every day for two years until it was as familiar as my fingernails; *Principles of Mathematics*, the advanced edition, but no longer advanced for me; *The Complete Adventures of Sherlock Holmes* in French, courtesy of Jeanne. There are other books, too, history and philosophy and art, and one very special book. It's a worn, illustrated story of *Cinderella*, with a gold-curlicued cover and heavy, old-fashioned images. I dreamed myself into those paintings every night of my childhood, and soaked up the words nearly every day. It's closer to me than my own name.

But even that now feels like too much.

Because suddenly I'm not sure I can go on being myself, while trying to do what's now ahead of me. I don't know how to be someone else, but I also know that the girl I was cannot exist outside the support of these walls.

No, I decide. I can't bear to hold on to these things from my old life. They have no place in my new one. I shove the box back under the bed.

With a last hug for my beloved second mother, I turn and leave my cell for the last time.

5

The prison gates clang shut behind me. The last guard retreats inside the block.

I am alone.

As I step out into the world, I feel it wobble around me. The wind blows down from the mountains, heavy with monsoon rain that has not yet fallen, even though we are near the brink of June. The clouds glower overhead, thick and strong as the prison gates at my back. But neither of them open for me. They just loom and look and do not move.

The road is dusty and the pavement is cracked, but I soon reach the spot where I am to meet Kiet the nephew. It's a faded gray bench by a post where a bus used to stop once, long ago. I drop onto the bench, clutching my tea box. I look around at this vast sweeping place, the world, and wonder what magic normal people see in it.

Emptiness, that's all I can see right now. Roads that lead to the mountains, mountains that scrape the sky. It's all strange and huge and wild. Of course, I have seen it all before, but that wasn't me; that was a girl with my same name, some creature of mud and bone who had never felt the lick of true freedom on her skin.

I still remember the first time I left the prison. How old was I—six? Seven? Isra spent weeks building me up to the big event, telling me stories of things we'd see and do, sneaking in tasty treats and telling me how much more there was "out there," walking me round and round the courtyard, pointing at distant spots and telling me what things were hiding just out of sight.

But when the gate creaked open and then shut behind me, and I looked back at Mama behind those bars, waving at me with her bright painted smile, I didn't know what all the fuss was about. Everyone seemed to be holding their breath, like they thought this trip might be too much for me. I just waved, and everyone sighed and went back to their day. And Isra sat me on the back of her bicycle and we rode off toward all those hidden things waiting to be discovered.

I didn't understand what I'd just done, not then. It took a little longer to realize that those of us on the inside couldn't just open the gates and walk out anytime we wanted. And once I did understand that, even though I still enjoyed the trips to the market and the overnight stays with Isra's family, it wasn't the same. Something inside me felt out of step after that. Some part of me knew I didn't fully belong in the real world.

Until now.

Because all those times going out with Isra are like rice paper to the silk of this now. Always, always before there was a tug in my belly, like a cord winding back to my cell, something inside me that could only rest behind the bars I called home. Now the cord has been cut, and the world outside is not the same one I traveled through before.

My legs are shaking so hard the old bench is starting to tremble in sympathy. I don't want this freedom, yet some part of it pulls at me. Does freedom have a taste? A smell? What is this tug that fights with my fear? I look away from the gates—and then I see my tree. How many nights I studied that gnarled tree from my cell—but how different it looks now, from here, as it squats lonesome in the midday sun. It should look bigger close up, but it doesn't. It looks small and stunted and weak. How will it ever weather the coming storm?

A cool breeze rushes down from the mountain and tosses my hair up off my forehead. And suddenly I know that freedom does have a smell. It is high and strong and sharp. It smells like danger. It smells alone. It is everything that is in the push of the air, right now, as the countryside waits for the great rain. Any moment now we will slide fast into flood and torrent.

The rain is late this year, but it has to come soon. And I am afraid that the longer it is held back, the harder it will fall.

I don't know if my tree will survive what is ahead.

6

There's a roar sawing through my silence for a long time before I see the thing that passes for a car in these parts. I may have grown up in a country prison in northern Thailand, but even I can tell that these four wheels should not be on the road. I think the car was red once, but that's just a guess.

The thing grinds to a stop, then has a coughing fit right in front of me, and the back left wheel falls off. The driver's door opens, slams shut, and a brisk skinny guy bursts into action all over the car. Kiet is busy with tools so shiny that either they've never been used before or they've yet to have a minute's rest. I have a feeling I know which. He is prying and lifting and poking and prodding, and meanwhile he jerks his head in my direction and calls to me in Thai.

I go a few steps closer. Kiet looks different than he did inside the prison. Out here, surrounded by sky and the wild world, he looks alien. My mind knows that I am safe with him, this nephew of my warden's, this boy I have known since before I could walk, but my pounding heart says I am getting into the car with a stranger.

I concentrate on what I know, to keep away the fear. Kiet is twenty and has lived in Bangkok for the last four years. He sends money back to his family, but prison gossip says he is there for the good life more than anything else. That he has become a city dweller. It has been a long time since the days we sat and played tic-tac-toe in white chalk on the prison floor. He is a boy I have known through the bars but now he is a man and I am not sure I know him anymore.

But he is heading back to Bangkok, with his car, and I have to admit the timing is excellent. Since I could be walking those seven hundred kilometers, I'm willing to live with my unease.

The car, too, is strange up close. I've read all about them in my old set of encyclopedias, and I've seen them on the little television set the guards put on for us sometimes in the evenings. Often, too, while out walking or riding on the back of Isra's bicycle I watched these metal beasts roar by. I always tried not to flinch, telling myself I had seen them many times and I knew all there was to know.

But here is what I now understand: seeing is different from knowing. What I have read about in my books and what I can touch with my hands are two very different things. I am afraid of this car and I am afraid of this big, strange world where I am now meant to belong.

Yet it's far too late to turn back.

After a few minutes Kiet looks in my direction, but then the stick that's supposed to be holding up the car cracks and the whole thing crashes down near his foot. He swears and gets back to work, and then I hear my name called out from behind me. From back inside the gates.

Something rises inside me like a mad joyful scream, and for a second I know, I just know that it's Mama standing there with that little scowl in between her eyebrows, wondering what took me so long to find her. I rocket back the way I came and throw myself at the gate.

But it's not Mama. Of course it's not; how can it be, when Mama is wrapped in bedsheet strips and tied around my neck? Still, it takes me a second to crash down from my high, dreamy place. I force myself to slow my breathing and smooth out my crooked expression, looking up at Jeanne, who stands behind the barred gate with eyes that tell me everything I don't want to hear.

We have always walked a narrow ledge, Jeanne and I, some fine boundary between resentment and grudging acceptance. She doled out equations and formulas like they were my due for taking up space in her world. And while I have chosen to hate the calculus rather than hating Jeanne, still I cannot ignore her altogether. But I will not let her see how she affects me.

I concentrate on keeping my breath level so nothing shows on my face. But Jeanne droops like a melting candle. I am surprised, and for a second my mask flickers.

She reaches through the gate and, after a second's hesitation, I put out my right hand to touch hers.

I feel it right away—the sheet of paper folded up so small it's like an extra flap of skin on her palm. The paper is thin and damp and I wonder if it's really there or if I'm just dreaming it.

"*Tiens, prends ça*," Jeanne says, and rattles on in French, telling me that this letter was sent to Mama years ago and Mama threw it out, but Jeanne found it and kept it because she is funny like that and has feelings about stuff that will be important, and now with the way things are she wants me to have it and who knows, it might be useful.

I swallow and cram my hand inside my pocket, then leave it there because I don't want to let go yet of that bit of Mama she tried so hard not to keep. I nod and start to turn away, but then Jeanne lunges forward, grabs my shoulder through the bars, and tugs at me. My cheek is up against the rusty metal and I can taste iron flecks on my tongue, but Jeanne holds on hard. I feel her breath on my earlobe. She is whispering fast and urgent.

"Listen careful, *ma petite*, I have to tell you something important. You know your *maman* had her ups and downs, yes?"

I wrench my shoulder from her grasp and pull my chin out of the gatework. My breath catches in my throat, but I make my voice steady. "Yes, what about it?" Mama's moods were legendary, long circuits from a pitch-black despair that slowly got better and better until I always thought this time, surely, everything would be okay. And then something would happen—I never knew what—to send her crashing back down, and the process would begin all over again.

Jeanne turned her head and looked to either side of herself, then lowered her voice further. "It was all because of her computer searches."

I looked at her blankly.

"Twice a year, they give us computer privileges. You know. I got them, and so did she. And one year, I notice something. I start watching Helena and observing what she does."

"Why? Why would you watch her?"

"*Quelle imbecile*, even you did not realize? Her black moods always started after her time on the computer. Then the weeks and months go by, she becomes happier, you think maybe she hopes again, yes? She starts to look out the window, talk about returning with you someday to America, yes? Then she goes on the computer, and her mood is midnight again."

I swallow. "I don't understand. What does that mean?"

Jeanne snorts. "I find out for you what it means. I pay off one of the guards, and here is what I learn—a long time ago I learn this, but what good would it ever do to say anything? Except now." She swallows. "Now you are leaving and who knows, maybe it will help you."

I can feel sweat pooling on my palms and my heart hammering in my chest. I want to be away, far away from

Jeanne and her schemes and manipulations. But nothing would move me from this spot.

"Every six months, your *maman* goes for her time on the Internet, and she looks up just one website. One place only she goes, the same every time: Payne Industries."

I wait, but Jeanne is silent now. "That's it? Payne Industries? What does that mean?"

"I don't know what it means, you fool. Only that it means something to your mother, and now I have told it to you, and I have done my duty. *C'est assez.* It is enough."

I'm still looking into her ice-blue eyes, trying to figure out what she means by all of this, if she really is trying to help me or if she has some other motive I don't understand, when Isra comes up behind Jeanne and taps her on the shoulder. With a shrug, Jeanne turns and walks back toward the cell block. Another part of my life that is gone forever. In spite of everything, I know I will miss her rough, grudging care.

And I don't even know what she has left me with. I file away my new knowledge to ponder at a later time and I smile at Isra, who reaches for me through the bars.

"I will miss you, little light," Isra says. I've been teaching her English, and she likes to practice with me. She's quite good, though she never believes me when I tell her. "We all will miss you. But you will do well in the world outside. Keep your head up and be strong."

I nod and try to smile because she wants me to, but I know my mouth looks like an old crumpled sock.

She's holding a black nylon duffel. "You forgot your things. I brought them to you. Your clothes and books and everything."

She slides open the zipper and there are my belongings, the ones I left under the bunk. I feel my breath catch in my throat. It was a split-second decision to leave it all behind, but from this side of the rusted iron gate I can hardly recognize those things. I can never belong to them again.

She starts to squeeze the bag through the bars and I find my voice.

"*Mai ao na kha*," I say, shaking my head and choking on my words because I want so badly for her to understand. "I don't want any of that stuff. It's not me anymore. I don't need it."

She doesn't understand, but how can I tell her that I am a worm born in a cave, that I need to grow my own wings in order to fly? How can I say that the girl who lived in cell block 413 and scrawled spelling words on the walls, who could conjugate verbs in three languages but who couldn't look up to follow a hawk's path across the sky, how can I make her see that girl is no longer me? These clothes belonged to that other person, but they have no part in my new journey. For this voyage I have other belongings, other clothing: the blanket of fear, the scarf of loneliness, the dark cloak of secrets. I have no room for anything else.

I'm saved from finding words by the roar of the engine behind me. Kiet's repairs have worked at last. Isra sighs in defeat and shoves a handful of *baht* at me. "Take this money at least," she says, and I can see she really means it, so after a second's pause, I do. My dollars will be of no use for getting around Bangkok, and I am grateful for her kindness.

I look hard into Isra's eyes, and the world stops. I see her younger, smiling, dancing with a tiny straw-haired girl, crooning *luk thung* ballads in my little ear. I see her drawing a *Tang Te* outline on the cement floor in chalk, showing me how to hop skillfully from one square to another, picking up the stone without ever putting my foot down. I see her head bent over my fifth-grade reader as she sounds out the words and tries to keep up with my translation in her halting English.

She has been a part of everything I've ever known. But now she is a part of my past.

My eyes smile and my hand that is still holding hers, with the money squashed inside, grasps on tightly. Then I let go, and I turn, and I don't say anything because since the day my mama left without saying it, *good-bye* is a word that no longer exists for me.

7

K iet opens the door for me, and I slide inside the car.
"*Pai nai?*" he asks with a smile.

The familiar phrase—literally asking where I am going,
but more of a welcome than a question—is our own special
greeting that I thought he'd have forgotten after all these
years. I look at him more closely. Inside that grown-up
face, the eyes of my childhood friend twinkle with mis-
chief. He's not so different after all.

"*Phuen,*" I whisper. Friend.

And he is.

Loosed from my fear, I'm free to examine everything
around me. And what a wonder it is! From the inside, this
beast is altogether different than it first seemed.

The seat is soft and crinkly, softer even than the five-
centimeter-thick mattress on my cot. Kiet starts talking
again, but I just look and look. Everywhere, all around, so
much to see! Buttons and knobs and handles—but above
all, light. I am surrounded by light. The window in front
of me is as big as the world, and there's more beside and

behind me. There is nothing, anywhere around, that I cannot see. It's like being outside, but safer. I can see the world, but it cannot get to me.

Then Kiet moves the gear shift and the car jumps forward. The movement hums through my body and sends my fear screaming back. Did I just think this metal box was *safe*? The motor coughs twice and starts to pick up speed.

I desperately want to clamp my eyes shut, to hold this moment in a dark bubble and block my view of the countryside that's now speeding by outside. But I force them to stay open. This is my world now. I must learn its ways.

Kiet turns to me with a lopsided smile, and I know he thinks he understands how I feel. He doesn't. How can he? But he is trying, and I am grateful.

"We'll take the old highway," he says, "the 106. It's slower going than the 11, but it's prettier."

I nod. This world here, now, is flying by—how could anything be faster?

My hands are squeezed into tight balls. I make myself unwrap them slowly, one finger at a time. I reach into my pocket and feel the paper Jeanne gave me. Mama's letter. I will not pull it out now, not with Kiet's eyes watching. I will read those words when they can fill the center of my mind for as long as I need them to.

"Luchi," says Kiet. "It's been a long time. Do you remember the games we used to play?"

I nod. "You were so tall," I say, then laugh because I sound like a child all over again.

But he grins. "I was sorry when my aunt thought I was too old to come and play."

That explains a lot. I'd always wondered why one day Kiet stopped visiting the cells. But in a prison filled with women, a fourteen-year-old boy would have been out of place. And not long after that, Kiet had left for Bangkok.

"One thing I've always wondered," he says now. "What does your name mean—Luchi? I've never heard it before."

I turn to my window. The happy flicker inside me hisses out and I remember where I am going, what I am setting out to do. "Light," I say. "Though it doesn't, really. Mama got it wrong. She thought the word meant light."

Kiet nods, as if accepting the tangle that was my mother's mind. I suddenly think of my naming as a frame for the rest of my mother's life. What other things did Mama assume, or come close to understanding, yet end up getting wrong? Is this another clue to the puzzle of my past, to all that she kept from me?

I could drown in these thoughts, so I'm happy when Kiet changes the subject. "You can open the window, you know."

Following his example I turn my handle in slow circles, enjoying the scritch-scratch sound and watching the window lower itself like an obedient subject. When it is all the way down, I put my elbow through the opening and lean my head out.

The wind grabs at my face and catches hold of my breath. I jerk back in and turn to Kiet, fighting the sudden sharp burst of joy. It doesn't fit with the turmoil of my thoughts. I don't want it, but it persists, dragging me into the core of the moment, filling me with a smile that pushes out onto my face.

Kiet is laughing. I return to the open window. My eyes eat up the countryside as it goes by. And suddenly . . . I feel at home. Tall bars line the road we are driving on, bars that shoot up into the sky as far as I can see. Out beyond are orchards and green rice fields, but all are framed by the comfort of the passing bars.

I lean my head back to look all the way up, and I realize the truth. "Those are trees?" I yell into the wind. "That tall?"

"Yes, the *yang na*," says Kiet. "Rubber trees. Aren't they amazing? There are nine hundred and three of them, planted more than a hundred years ago. There's a number on each one."

I can't see the numbers; we're moving too fast. And I can't think of them as trees. It makes me happy to feel there are still some bars—wide enough to slip through, but strong enough to stand guard for me, though I am set loose into the world.

"Lamphun," Kiet says, waving at a city just coming into view. "We're at the provincial boundary. This is where the *yang na* end."

I can see it now, the gaping hole up ahead where the tall bars stop, where the empty world circles, waiting for me. My eyes fill with tears and I stretch my hand toward the last trees that are flying by my window.

The outside is different, too. Something is changing. A low drumming sound starts in the distance and builds until I can hear it loud over the motor of the car. Then I feel it: a fat drop splatters on my outstretched palm. I rub my fingers together to savor the cool wetness. Another drop licks my fingertips. In five seconds, my hand is damp.

"Stop," I whisper into the wind, and somehow Kiet hears me because he swerves off to the side, ignoring the screeches and honks behind us. We ride up onto the grass and I fling open my door and fall out.

We have stopped next to the last tree, and I stand by it with my head bowed.

And the rains come at last.

They pour down on me with all the force and fury of a pent-up storm. I know Kiet is sitting inside the car, watching me, not understanding. But I don't care. I am alone in a world of water, swimming in the tears of the sky.

I let it consume me. I am water inside and out. The rain draws up all my sorrow and brings it bubbling to the surface. And now, finally, I can let loose the thunderstorm inside me. I cry for Mama. I cry for Bibi and Jeanne and Isra. I cry for the last *yang*, the last bar that I will now have to leave behind.

And I cry for the wide-open space ahead of me, the

great unknown that wants to swallow me whole. I cry until I look up and I realize that I cannot see the city ahead, Lamphun, anymore. The sheeting rain is blocking it from view.

Then I know I have cried enough. I don't want my tears to block my view of what's ahead. I am terrified, but I am determined.

I must go forward.

8

Kiet looks at me and my open window. We are driving again, and he says the rain will drown the car. There is a river around my feet and the seat under me sloshes like laundry. Kiet flips a switch and little gusts of air start to blow on me. But they will not dry me while I have the outside pouring in through my window. And I can't bear to close it.

My tears are gone, but I love the feel of the sky on my skin.

I wonder if Kiet will be angry with me, but he just laughs. "The car will not dry out until the end of the rainy season anyway," he says.

I keep my hand outside the window, watching every drop patter across my palm. Growing up I didn't like to bathe—the big open room, with so many women coming in and out. But a bath like this I could learn to enjoy.

Now Kiet rolls down his own window and the rain pours in on his short-cropped hair, soaking his orange T-shirt. He flashes me a wide smile. "I should get used to being out in the rain," he tells me. It is the kind of sentence that starts a story, and I don't have to wait long to find out more.

"I am driving to Bangkok to *buat phra*. I will be ordained as a monk at the Wat Suwannaram."

I try to imagine Kiet in the saffron robes of a monk. It does not fit the picture my mind has built around the prison gossip of the careless, irresponsible youth. Of course, from that same gossip I know he did *poi san long* when he was younger than I am now. Many boys perform this ceremony before they reach their teen years, taking up the robes as novices for weeks or months at a time. But to go fully into the life of a monk shows a greater commitment to making spiritual merit. From all I have heard, the life of a *Bhikkhu* is not easy. I look at Kiet curiously. What has pushed him in this direction?

Kiet sees me staring and laughs. "You are surprised."

"No!" I won't admit it.

"You should be. It is a big change of path for me." He grins. "You should have seen my aunt's face when I told her."

"Why?" The word slips out almost before I realize it is coming, but suddenly I have to know. How can someone change so completely, become so different than who he was—how did Kiet do it? How did he even know it could be done? I turn to face him, desperate for this knowledge, but his eyes are on the road; his words, when they come, do nothing for me.

"It was time," is all he says.

But what more can he say? He has found his road. He is moving toward his shelter.

And I am moving away from mine.

9

We leave the highway and drive into Lamphun, because Kiet says we need to stop for food. I reach into my pocket and finger the crumpled *baht* that Isra gave me. It's no use pulling the money out; Kiet will not accept it. As my elder he will naturally pay for my food. It would be rude for me even to offer. I know this, but I still feel uncomfortable. All my life on the inside I have been cared for, all my needs met by my elders. Is this how it will always be, even now that I am out?

These thoughts fill my mind until the moment we pull in to the city center. Then, all is forgotten. Despite the rain, Lamphun is crawling like an anthill. I can see that it is market day, and my heart speeds up. So many faces, so many moving feet, so many strangers all in one place!

Kiet stops the car on the side of a street opposite the stalls. The cloth awnings all look mud brown through the downpour, but they are thick and allow the townspeople to move easily among the booths without getting too wet. From my spot I can see vegetables and fruits, meat and fish of all types. I can see basket sellers and toy makers and cobblers and craftsmen with fancy carved vases.

Kiet's fingers curl, and I can see he is eager to go out among them. But I am frozen in place.

"Come," says Kiet. "There is a stall I know well. They make the best food and will give us a good price."

The crowds throng past the car, people moving and pushing, full of their own life, owning their space in the world. These people know who they are, I'm sure, every one of them. I don't know how to walk with these people and pretend I am one of them. I don't feel real enough.

Inside, I'm still a girl made of paper.

"Come," Kiet says again.

I shake my head. All words are gone, there is just my heart pumping with a nameless panic. My hands are mashed into my seat.

Kiet nods. "Wait here, then. I will be back."

He shuts his door and moves off toward the market. The moment he is gone, I lean over and roll his window shut. I do the same with mine. Now I cannot feel the rain, but the noise of the crowd is lower, too. I want to close my eyes, to cover the sight of all this foreign chaos as easily as I muffled its sound. I shove my hands deep into my pockets.

And there I feel the familiar scrap of paper.

I pull out the worn sheet that Jeanne kept in secret for so long. The letter Mama wanted to throw away. It is damp from my pocket, and I open it carefully. The handwriting is choppy and unfamiliar. I read slowly, trying to put extra meaning into every word.

Mrs. Regina Finn
21 Stafford Circle
Brookline, Massachusetts
USA

August 29

Dear Helena,

I write these words as I have written so many before, sending them out to so many different places, hoping against hope that they will find their way to you. Yet with each unanswered letter I feel another beat of that hope flying from me. Where are you, my darling? Where in the world could you be? Are you even still alive to read these words, should one of my letters search you out and find where you have hidden? Only my heart tells me that you are alive, my heart that knows you better than I know myself, my heart that would sense a world where you no longer lived.

We have all heard the horrifying news, and I want you to know that I will stand by you in this. Won't you tell me what really happened? You know that monster of a man will twist any tale to his advantage, will manufacture his own truth, and I

know there is more to the story than we are being
told.

Please, my darling, come home and let me help
you. I am waiting every day for news of your
return. Don't stay away any longer!

With love and prayers and hope that this letter
will find you,

Mom

By my tenth reading I've chased my thoughts in circles
and am no nearer to catching them. I have always accepted
Mama's life, her decision to cut herself off from her past.
And it was her choice; after all, other foreign prisoners
received calls from their embassies, letters and parcels from
home, visits from family and friends. None of these for
Mama. No, she lived under some nameless fear, some private terror in which the outside world was more to be feared
than our own confinement. I think again of the company
Jeanne told me about: Payne Industries. Did this place
have anything to do with Mama's fear, as Jeanne suspected?
Mama never said a word about it to me—or to anyone,
apparently. We just remained hidden behind the bars that
she saw not as a prison but as a protection. Her ups and
downs set the tempo of our lives, winding us around in a
rhythm none of us could see.

It is what I have grown up with. It is the known and the
safe and the understood. But if Mama was not alone—nor
unwanted—then what were her reasons for keeping so far

away from her past? What was the cause of her terror? Why did she bury herself in secrets?

My mama had a mother. This much, of course, I always knew at some level. But looking at the page now, holding it in my hand, sends my whole body trembling. Beyond the mysteries and the questions, beyond the unnamed horrifying event, beyond this monster man who maybe caused my mama to retreat from her world—apart from all that, there is something else.

In this world—this big, empty, lonely world—there is a woman whose heart knew Mama's better than her own, a woman who loved her in spite of everything else. My mama's mother.

My grandmother.

10

⁂

By the time Kiet returns, I have started to get used to the idea that I may not be completely alone in the world.

This knowledge has also given me a larger plan. I will still travel to Bangkok, but now with a greater purpose. From there I will—I must—reach America, to find this woman, my grandmother. Surely she will have the answers I seek.

So when Kiet swings open his door, I fold the paper away and look at him with a hopeful smile. He is dripping, though the rain seems to have slowed, and he holds two wooden bowls draped with palm leaves. He pushes one into my hands and the smell curls out to meet me. There are flat noodles with chunks of chicken and dots of peanuts and bean sprouts mixed all through. The scent of chili makes my mouth water. I pull out the small fork and tug hot noodles into my mouth.

"You have eaten pad thai before?" Kiet asks, sitting down next to me and beginning his own meal.

I nod, though it was only once, many years ago, while out with Isra. And this meal is as different from the food I ate on the inside as the Toyota advertisement on television is from this car I sit in, as different as the gossip tales told of Kiet are from this strange, kind man by my side. I wonder if everything feels more real outside the walls of the Khon Mueang Women's Prison.

And then I push all other thoughts away and sink into my meal.

A half hour later, Kiet has returned the bowls to the street vendor and come back into the car. He hands me a paper bag, and when I peek inside I see several mandarin oranges, two coconut cakes, and a newspaper-wrapped package of sticky yellow jellies. He tells me I can open those now and I do, offering him some, but he just shakes his head and starts up the car.

I smile and begin to eat, continuing until the jellies are almost gone. The kilometers fly by as we set Lamphun behind us and follow the provincial highway south. I am proud of how easy it feels now to ride in a car. The rain is falling again, but I am happy to watch it through closed windows.

"The rain makes the ride slower, and we got a late start in any case," says Kiet. "Tonight, we will stay with my cousins. They live not far from Sukhothai. It is on our way."

I nod, but my stomach clenches. It is nothing to Kiet, who knows them already, but for me a house of strange cousins will be harsh and new. I tell myself that everyone is a stranger to me now, and that the experience of meeting new people has to begin sometime. Kiet looks at me sideways and seems to be having the same thought. But his eyes soften with understanding. Maybe he sees my lips press into a thin line, or the last yellow jelly that is squished flat inside my palm.

He reaches out to the dashboard and pushes a round button, and music fills the car. It's a wonder! One second I am hiding from my thoughts in the silence, and the next, the music wraps itself around me like a warm blanket, rocking me like Bibi's loving arms.

"There is a radio in your car!" I exclaim in delight. It seems hard to believe, that the notes could ring so loud and clear in this tiny space. I almost think I am back on my cot with Isra's headphones in my ears. But this is so much better. It brings to life the greenery that flies by my window.

I lean back in my seat and close my eyes. Now the music itself is like a living thing, and I let it reach out a hand and grab my inner fear, that skinny coward that trembles in the corner. The music twirls and prods until the fear, too, starts to dance, starts to forget all about the dark and everything ahead, losing itself completely in music and light and warmth.

I am still dancing as I drift into sleep.

11

When I open my eyes, the car has stopped. The music is gone. I am alone.

Through the rain-drenched windows I can see a wide wall of dark teak wood. I lean forward and rub a circle in the fog on the window, trying to see out. A cluster of people stand in the downpour outside the house. In the center of that group is Kiet. His orange T-shirt is like a lucky charm that everyone seems to want to reach out and touch. I can hear his laughter from where I sit, safe behind my tightly closed doors.

After a few minutes his head turns in my direction and my safe feeling slips away as he runs toward the car. He flings open the door. "Come out, Luchi," he calls, and his eyes are sparkle-bright. His smile looks big enough to swallow me up, if I'd only let it. But I'm trembling too hard to try.

"Everyone is gathering," he says gently, leaning over and reaching a hand in my direction. "They are making a feast and have invited all the family from the village. It will be a party!"

I lower my head and swallow the lump in my throat. I know I need to get out and so I do, but my eyes only slide from one mud puddle to the next. I follow the tracks left by Kiet's sandaled feet, watching the rain poke holes in the muddy surface. My soaked hair makes a curtain in front of my eyes. I do not lift a hand to move it away, even though there are mutters and muffled greetings around me.

Perhaps Kiet has prepared them. Perhaps they can tell by my posture that I am new in their world, that I am not ready to meet a group of strangers. Whatever the reason, I move through the crowd like I am still behind my tightly shut windows. No one tries to pull me into a conversation. I am grateful for this, though I'm ashamed at my rudeness.

Then a strong hand clasps my elbow and a wiry voice speaks almost in my ear. *"Kin khao laew rue yang?"* Have you eaten yet? The familiar greeting, which is more about comfort and safety than about food.

It has happened. I am no longer invisible. I stop and mumble a reply, bringing my numb hands together as I lower my head in a respectful *wai*. But after this traditional gesture, to my surprise I am not called on to meet more people. Instead the arm begins to guide me, moving me past clusters of muddy feet, up a row of rough-hewn stairs, and onto the porch. At the door I kick off my plastic sandals and try to scuff away the worst of the mud. The hand reaches down into a ceramic water pot and pulls out a long wooden dipper. Water splashes all over my feet. I dry them on the cloth mat and step into the house.

The door shuts behind us.

Now that we are alone, I lift my eyes from the floor and look into the face of my guide. She is wrinkled like an old cloth, but her eyes remind me of Bibi. I try out the traditional name I have never had cause to use before: *Khun yai*. Grandmother. Yai grabs my hand and tugs me farther inside the house. We move from the main room into a second, smaller one. There is a wide open floor and a few pieces of furniture scattered around the edges.

Leaving me at the door, Yai crosses the room and pulls out a rolled-up mat made of finely woven rushes. She unrolls this along the ground and covers it with a few pieces of bedding.

"*Nang long na ja.*"

I follow her directions and make myself comfortable on the mat.

Then she points to a door on the far side of the room and continues: "The washroom is there. You can clean up, and I will bring you food soon. Take some time for peace in here."

Her words loosen the tangled knot inside me. I think she sees this, because she nods and smiles. "Who wants to be in a noisy room full of strangers right away? When you feel ready, you can come and join us. Tonight or tomorrow—it doesn't matter. You take all the time you need."

She gives me one last smile, then turns and goes out. Through the closed door I can hear tromping feet, noisy laughing voices as the party moves inside. Smells of curry and roasting fish creep under the door.

Later, other mats will be rolled out, and the room will fill up with sleeping bodies. Later, a tray heaped with good food will be brought to me by a kind soul who understood the needs I could not express. Later I will wash and crawl, clean, into my bedding.

But for now I am content to stand here, alone, in this small corner of tranquillity, in this house brim full of laughter, overflowing with family.

Long minutes pass before the room stops pulsing around me, before my quiet laps over into the rest of my surroundings. But finally I return to myself.

And now I puzzle over the problem of washing. I look down at my damp, sweaty shirt, my mud-stained shorts. How can I clean my body and then return to these clothes? For the first time I consider the effect of leaving behind all my belongings.

Then I see, among the bedding that Yai has left behind, some pink flowered cloth. A sarong. My eyes water at this unexpected kindness. Did she see that I had brought no spare clothing with me? Or did Kiet tell her?

I pick up the cloth and hold it to my cheek. It feels like a flower petal.

Now I am ready. I push open the door to the washroom and step inside. It is a new feeling to pull off my clothing in the small, private space, so different from the large prison washroom. Setting my muddy clothes in a pile, I reach trembling hands to the big wooden dipper, dump the cool water over my body, and begin to scrub away the last of the mud from my first life. The water dripping off me starts dull brown and gradually becomes clearer and lighter.

I wonder if it could really be that easy, slipping out of one skin and into another, becoming someone different, someone altogether new. If only I could wash away my past as easily as the hard prison soil.

It's worth a try.

Slowly, slowly the last of the water swirls away down the drain. Finally I stand up, and I wrap myself in this gift from a stranger, this gift as soft as kindness, as warm as acceptance, as quiet as peace.

I still don't know exactly who I am, but I am wonderfully warm and dry and alone, and for now, that is enough.

12

The music and the celebration continue, and before long Yai returns with a bamboo tray. There is a dish of steaming rice, and five little bowls filled with sauces and toppings. My mouth waters as I gratefully accept the tray from her hands.

From the far room comes the sound of voices erupting in laughter. The door opens and a woman pokes her head in. Her forehead is shiny with sweat and her eyes are dancing. But those same eyes pass over me quickly, uncertainly. She tells Yai that everyone is waiting on her for a story, then goes quickly back the way she's come. Yai hesitates, and her gaze flicks toward the main room. I can see it tugging at her, calling her back.

I make a half turn away, releasing her from any obligation to stay, eager in any case to sink into my meal.

The old woman sighs and smiles, and there is nothing unsure in the way her gaze holds me. She does not ask if I want to go back in the main room with her, and I do not offer.

"You will be well," she says. "It will take time. But you are becoming well already."

I nod and swallow at the lump in my throat. I do not know what to say to this, so I use the little curved spoon to ladle some fish sauce onto my rice.

After another minute, she turns toward the door. "You look good in this sarong. I sewed it myself and wore it for many years." She laughs softly. "It is too bright for an old woman. I will be pleased if you keep it."

"*Khob khun kha*," I thank her, and I am not only speaking of the sarong. In her eyes I see a flash of something— kindness? Understanding? Sympathy? I can't identify it, and it's gone in the next blink. Perhaps I imagined it. With another smile, Yai leaves me with my meal.

Oh, the food! I fall upon it with a passion that is brand-new. Inside, our meals were carefully scheduled: every day at the same time, in the same place, routine upon routine. There was one dish planned for each meal of the week, unchanged by passing weeks, months, and years. The food was pleasant, and it filled my stomach. When there were bugs or tiny stones in the rice, we picked them out and thought nothing of it. When the fish gave off a sour smell, there was always more sauce to cover it up.

But this—nothing has prepared me for this glory. The scent rolls over me and I lean my head forward, soaking in the steaming heat, afraid to take a bite and break the spell. Finally I can't wait any longer and I dig my fork into the rice.

Once I start, I cannot stop. Bite follows bite, food hot and savory and spicy and flavorful in a way that fades every other food I have eaten into memories of dust. At last I put the empty tray on the floor next to me and fall back on my woven rush mat, exhausted.

My stomach is full, my eyes are heavy, and I am content.

13

I open my eyes, and the house is dark around me. Dark and quiet. When did I fall asleep? I am still lying on my back, but the bamboo tray is gone. Someone has pulled a light cover on top of me. The room is filled with the steady hum of quiet breaths drawing in and out, in and out. Rain drums on the high roof like a heartbeat—soft, steady, and continuous.

It is my first night alone on the outside. I had imagined lying awake with an empty heart and trembling nerves; instead, I am full to the brim with food and comfort. My eyes drift shut, but I tug them open. This is a moment, now, that has never come to me before. I am the owner of my time. The night belongs only to me. There are no bars surrounding this bed.

I sit up, slide my legs off the side of the mat. Above my head, the blades of the ceiling fan hum, stirring my need for adventure. I pad my bare feet across the floor, step carefully around mats and crumpled covers, through the half-open door, past the kitchen, and out onto the front porch.

The rain beats down in a fine sheet, so I don't move from the wooden steps. I sit and draw my knees to my chest. There is nowhere I want to go in this downpour, but I revel in the blurred night landscape. Right now, this minute, I could go anywhere I please. I am no one. I am everyone. I am anything I want to be. A smile spreads across my face.

Then a scuffle behind me makes me turn my head. The front door opens and I see a small round face, beetle-black eyes. A girl no taller than my waist patters out and comes to sit next to me.

We sit in silence, and I steal glances at her out of the corner of my eye. Her two long braids are tossed and scuffed, like they have been fighting with her pillow. Her eyes are crusted with sleep, and once she yawns like a tired bird. I smile, and she sees it, and her face lights like a sunbeam.

"I am Pensri," she lisps. "Who are you?"

"Luchi," I say.

"Your hair is a strange color."

I grin and her forehead wrinkles, like she just realized what she said. She goes on quickly. "But it's a nice color. I like it. I wish my hair was that color, too."

"Your hair is beautiful," I tell her. "Like the midnight sky."

That makes her smile. "How long will you stay? My *mae* says you are a visitor and should not be bothered."

"You aren't bothering me." I pause, then surprise myself by adding, "I like it here. I like you."

Pensri pulls her tiny hands into a *wai*, lowers her head

respectfully. "You will be my older sister, then. *Phee sao.* May I call you that?"

A glow warms my chest. "Of course, *nong sao.* Little sister."

Pensri yawns again. "I will go back to bed, then. See you tomorrow, *phee sao.*"

And she is gone.

I wait a few minutes, looking out at the rain and the dark, friendly night. Then I get up and follow her back into the sleeping room. In seconds I lose myself to sleep, and do not stir again until daybreak.

14

Morning comes early to this house on the edge of the forest. Before the sun is all the way up on the rain-soaked horizon, women and girls are bustling around me, folding sheets and rolling up mats. I let myself be tossed like a twig in the river of their busyness, moving and folding and packing as best I can. No one speaks to me. I keep my eyes on the floor and try to copy what I see others doing.

Pensri steals glances and smiles my way, and I smile back. Khun Yai is nowhere to be seen. But I listen as I work, and though no one speaks to me, there is much to be learned. I discover that Yai is a cousin of Kiet's grandmother. She lives in this house along with her son and his wife and their five daughters. Pensri is the youngest of these girls, and doted upon by all.

The many guests of the night before have returned to their homes, but the house still feels comfortably full. After a while everyone drifts into the kitchen, and when I step through to follow them, I find the family scrunched around the breakfast table. The men are there, too, and Kiet throws me an enthusiastic smile and makes room next to him. I slide gratefully into the seat.

The room is abuzz with life. Hands dart across the table, pulling and grabbing and poking. Kiet, too, is full of loud morning confidence. He makes a great show of swatting others aside and helping himself to the choice toppings. Then he passes the dishes on to me. I eat my rice in silence, reflecting on the strange, strong way people on the outside move through life. I try to decide what the difference is. On the inside, people looked the same. We spoke the same words. We laughed and cried and sighed like any other people. There were bars on the windows, but there were no bars on the soul.

Or were there? Inside, everything was routine, planned, predictable. On the outside, you have the sense that on any given day, anything might happen—wonderful or terrible, but quite often unexpected. Anything might happen to bring some change to what is up ahead.

And now, suddenly, it does.

His mouth half-full of fish, Kiet looks toward Yai and announces: "I have learned that the road out has been closed from all the rain. They have shut down the only way onto the highway. We will need to stay here a few more days, if you will allow us."

I look up from my rice bowl in time to see a glance pass across the table. I can imagine worse things than having to stay longer in this peaceful home. But what do our hosts think of it? I study their faces and try to decide.

Khun Yai merely inclines her head. Pensri's mother tightens her lips into a thin smile. Pensri's father lifts his hand jovially. "Of course! As long as you need to. Our home is your home."

My throat feels tight. There is welcome in this offer, certainly, but something else, too. Something more shadow than afternoon sun. Some hesitation that will never be voiced but which I cannot keep from hearing.

"How long will the road stay closed?" I whisper.

Kiet turns his eyes away from me. "It cannot be for long. And it will be good for you to stay here. See how glad they are to have you around!"

Yai and the others are now flinging exclamations of delight around the room at the prospect of this unexpected stay. But my stomach feels knotted. Some part of me is grateful to have added time before I must face the big city. But what is this undercurrent I feel, so different from the words being spoken? I blush with shame at the forced hospitality that I have no way of refusing.

Still, what must be must be. The sound of the rain on the high wooden roof rings out like hollow laughter. Is the sky mocking my predicament? I lift my head and, carefully, meet Yai's gaze.

"I am pleased to remain here longer," I say. "You have made me feel so welcome. I would have been sorry to leave so soon."

Yai nods and I return to my meal.

Then a thin voice pipes up. "I am glad you are staying longer, *phee*. I want you to stay forever!"

And the room freezes. The adults stop, mouths half-open, spoons half-raised. All heads turn to look at Pensri, who breaks into a wide smile.

"She does not mind if I speak to her, *Khun Mae*," the little girl tells her mother. "We talked last night and she was very friendly. She said I could be her *nong sao*."

There's a ripple in the air, then, and for a second the sunny warmth blinks out altogether. Pensri's mother leans in and whispers in the girl's ear, while the others exchange uncertain looks. Only Kiet acts as though nothing is wrong, tossing casual conversation out into the crowd until, slowly, the others also begin to smile and talk. And everything seems to return to normal.

But it doesn't, really. Because I can't help but notice that Pensri is no longer smiling. Her eyes are fixed on the table.

She does not say another word to me for the rest of the afternoon. And something tells me that yesterday's breath of perfect contentment will not return to me anytime soon.

15

The next days crawl by. With the rain still coming down in torrents, no one goes out to work in the rice fields. Instead, floors are scrubbed, stairways are repaired, clothes are patched and sewn.

I help out where I can, but I seem to do everything wrong. No one says anything, but several times I catch Yai rescrubbing a floor I just finished, or quietly returning my washed dishes to the bottom of the tub. And still, the sugared kindness is heaped on me until I could scream.

Why, for once, cannot someone tell me the truth, what they are really thinking?

All day I look around for Pensri, remembering the warm feel of her unconditional acceptance. But she has almost completely disappeared. Every morning, after a silent breakfast, she vanishes to parts unknown and I don't see her for the rest of the day. At night, her rush mat is on the farthest side of the room from mine. And though I creep out to watch the rain every night, there is never a patter of feet behind me to say I am not alone.

I am alone. I am still that girl in cell block 413. The bars are invisible now, but one thing is certain: as long as they exist in people's memories, they exist. Apparently, the warning Pensri received about speaking with me was for her sake rather than mine. After all, who knows what strange habits and behaviors I might bring with me from such a dire place?

It must be as I suspected: I am not a suitable big sister for a child. She cannot be my *nong sao*.

I push away the hurt. It does not matter. I will be gone from here, just as soon as the rain lets up.

But let it come quickly.

More tolerable are the long evenings when music whips wildly around the main gathering room. Khun Yai is the only one in the house who has continued to treat me with a steady acceptance. She redoes my chores around the house, yes, for obviously I have little practice in the ways of this household. But she never accuses me with her eyes, never watches me as though something might go wrong at any moment.

On these long, rainy nights I sit with the women and work on my first piece of needlework. Yai has given me a square of cream-colored cloth and told me I may use any colors of thread from the rainbow in her basket. She shows me how to poke the needle so gently into the fabric, pulling it in and out to form neat little lines that, when put all together, will make a picture.

I pull on my needle, following the call of the colors, the feel of the cloth. Yai looks at my work. She smiles.

"Do you have a picture in mind?" she asks.

I look at my square. The colors streak this way and that, with no visible pattern or direction, brown and green meshed together in a strong, wild tangle. I nod uncertainly. "There is a picture here, but I don't yet know what it is."

"It will come to you," she says. "You bring the color, and the pattern will appear."

With a nod, Yai returns to her own work. This may be as close as we ever come to communication, for while she does not shun me, I can see she will not go against the grain of her family with an active friendship. Again I think of Mama and all the things that were not said. And I see how easy it would be to build a life of small, easy silences.

I see this, but I do not agree.

Outside, the rain beats and beats, and I turn my mind to the sky, to the road, willing the rain to pause, for the way out to open for me soon. I long to be away from this tangle of tightly stitched people, this core of belonging that has no room for me.

I fear behind these invisible bars I might lose myself all over again, might let slip through my fingers this small piece of myself I am just beginning to discover.

16

On the fourth day, the rain slows enough that I decide to go out for a walk. Kiet offers to come along but I shake my head, pleased with my growing power to choose my own way.

"I will just walk around the back," I say. "The air is fresh, and I want to be alone."

He nods in agreement and I walk into the kitchen, where Yai is sorting beans with Pensri's mother. Yai looks up, then tilts her chin toward a hat that is resting on the kitchen table. "Take this," she says. "It will keep off the rain." I can feel their watchful eyes as I shut the front door behind me.

I expect to find my plastic sandals stiff and hard with caked mud. Instead, someone has washed them clean and set them neatly under the eaves. With mingled shame and gratitude, I slide them onto my feet and pad down the steep wooden stairs.

The air is balmy and warm, and the light rain patters friendly fingers across the wide woven hat. I pull the string from the end of my long braid, tugging until my hair falls loose around my shoulders. A lot of the cloying heat has been washed out of the air, and I drink the freshness in wide gulps.

Mud puddles dot the yard and I step around each one, making a game out of choosing a path through this watery maze. At every turn I face a new decision. Right or left? Around the pineapple-shaped puddle, or over the skinny loopy one? I lose myself in this game of choice, loving the way my feet follow exactly where I want them to go and that it is me, all me, directing the events.

Before I know it, I have reached the end of the yard. I turn back to look at the house, which looms high off the wet ground on wooden posts. No one is on the porch. There is nobody checking to see what I might do. I think of the many watchful eyes that policed my every move on the inside, and I feel giddy at my own power.

I turn my back to the house and push through the barrier of trees that ring the property.

The forest is like a big green pocket that I have fallen into. Trees, vines, bushes, branches—there is greenery everywhere. I have never seen so many plants in one place. The rain cannot reach me through the leafy covering, but there is a steady *plop-plop-plop* of bigger drops gathering on the plantain leaves above me, collecting into miniature pools, then sending wet surprises tumbling down my back.

A trail leads into the woods and I walk along it,

soaking in the wonder around me. Between the plants and the lush wildlife, I almost miss the noise at first. Then it comes again—indistinct but unmistakable, and getting closer.

The sound of voices.

Speaking in English.

Without stopping to think, I duck off the path. I squat down and pull a leafy bush in front of my face. Then I part the leaves just enough to peer through. I don't have long to wait. Around the bend in the road strides a tall, gangly man. His face is red and sweaty, and his breath comes in short puffs. The pack he's carrying towers over his head. Right behind him is a young woman, maybe the same age as Isra but with skin as pale as coconut milk. Two braids of red hair brush her shoulders. Her face, unlike her companion's, is fresh and clear, and wears a teasing smile. She is whistling.

"Tam! Will you stop that already?" the man barks.

I shrink farther back in the bushes, but his voice is more exasperated than angry.

"Wait, wait," Tam replies. "I'm just getting to the good part." She whistles louder and scoots along the path, now shoving her shoulder into her companion. He stumbles and nearly falls, rights himself, then stops in the middle of the trail, hands on his hips.

They are just a few paces from my hiding spot, and I watch with wide eyes. How strange it is to hear this exchange in English! How strange, for that matter, to hear

English spoken by anyone other than Mama. It was always our special language, our secret language. Though I'm sure some others inside must also have spoken it as well, I never felt Mama wanted me to search them out. It was just another thing she liked keeping to herself.

These strangers' voices sound different, though. The words are like rubber bands, stretching and twanging in unusual places. I hope they will talk more, but they just stand glaring at each other. Or rather, the man glares, and the woman—Tam—stands there smirking. I notice how under his gaze she puffs out her chest, lifts her head, pulls her shoulders straighter. She raises her eyes until they are level with his. Then she slowly licks all the way around her lips, curls them into an O—and starts to whistle again.

I can't help it. I am so transported by this exchange that I let out a startled laugh. It comes out halfway between a gasp and a shriek, once I realize what I have done and am too late to take it back. The shock sends me sprawling backward into the bush, and my feet slip on the wet ground.

There is a scuffle out on the trail, but my leafy curtain has fallen and I cannot see the couple. I pull my feet back inside the shrubs from where they had slid out.

"Hey, d'you hear that?" comes the man's voice. It is facing in my direction now. He sounds wavering and unsure.

"Heard and *saw*," says Tam, and her voice is very close. I wonder if I should run away—but going off the trail into the forest is too risky. "Two sandaled feet, yes I did—and if I'm not mistaken, they were right about . . . *here!*"

With that word, the cluster of growth in front of me is yanked away and I see Tam's face, very close, like a hunter checking on a trap. But seeing me so near must surprise her because she jumps back a step, letting the bush snap into place. I hear the scrabbling of feet and low voices conferring out on the trail.

I know what I need to do. They've already seen me—and after all, what do I have to lose?

Standing up, I pat my hair and smooth my clothes, making sure everything is in place. Then I push aside the bushes and step out.

There is a moment of shocked silence. I stand facing them, and they look at me with turtle gawps. Finally Tam clears her throat.

"Well, hi there. You just out for a walk in the bush or something?" She hesitates. "You, uh, speak English?" The words shoot from her mouth so sharp and quick it's all I can do just to keep up.

"Yes, I do," I say.

Tam frowns. "Where're you from, then? You've got a different accent from any I've heard. Oh—" She laughs, and juts out her hand. "I'm Tamara Zus, by the way. And this is my mate Paul. We're from Sydney."

I look at her hand, unsure what to do. Finally I take a guess and put my hand out alongside hers. She gives me an odd look, then grabs my hand and squeezes hard. I gasp a little, but she is smiling, so I squeeze back. I am not used to touching hands like this, but her grasp is firm and warm, and I can feel the friendship-squeeze run all the way down to my toes.

Paul puts his hand out next. Now that I know what to do, the squeeze does not catch me by surprise. His hand is too big, though, and sticky with sweat.

"So," says Tam, "you were talking about what you're up to out here in the wilderness. Not trekking the country alone at your age!"

I know that I look young, and I shake my head quickly. "No. I am visiting friends. They live near here." It's getting easier to talk to these easygoing foreigners, but a life on the inside has taught me caution. I wonder how much I should tell them about myself. And then it comes to me, a warm gush of realization. These people—these strangers— know nothing about me. They will know only what I tell them. To them, I am not an oddity, a girl who has grown up in prison, who has lived behind bars every day of her life. To them, I am normal.

I am whoever I say I am.

Understanding breaks over my face in a smile. So this is how I can begin again, how I can become new. I just need to distance myself from my past. Leave it behind once and for all.

I look up to meet Tam's eyes. "I was born here, in a city up north. I'm traveling with a friend—his family lives nearby. I just came out for a walk."

Tam and Paul don't even blink at my story. It's all true, of course, but I'm amazed at how those few omissions make my life sound so ordinary.

"Yeah, well, we've been trekking since yesterday morning," says Paul. "We drove up on Monday and we've been staying in the village, trying out the trails. Bad time of year for this kind of adventuring, that's what I say." He shakes his head and throws a scowl in Tam's direction.

But I am suddenly confused. Monday? The day before yesterday? "How did you drive in to the village on Monday? The road has been closed since Saturday morning."

Tam frowns. "The road's not closed, love. We've been in and out three times since we got here."

The conversation around me fades. All I can hear is my heartbeat thudding in my ears. I turn abruptly and start back down the path the way I came. I can hear Paul and Tam calling out behind me, but I don't stop. If the road is no longer closed, why hasn't Kiet told me? This very morning, in fact, he said we were still shut in.

And now another thought freezes my blood, as the forest flies past my now running feet.

Was the road ever shut down at all?

By the time I reach the porch stairs, the buzz in my head has swelled to a typhoon. Swirling emotions storm through me. On the landing I kick off my sandals and unclench my trembling hands. My cheeks feel hot. My breath comes in short gasps. I am fighting for air after running so fast, but something inside me is fighting, too. I feel a pushing in my chest, like something trying to break through a wall or a barrier.

Before I can go in, Kiet opens the front door. He looks surprised to see me.

"Luchi," he says. "I was just coming out to look for you."

I glower at him and struggle against my growing anger. Mama had a fiery temper—more than once growing up I saw her fly into a fury over something Jeanne said or did. But all the years on the inside—or perhaps Thailand itself—eventually tamed her. Public outbursts are simply not done. "*Jai yen yen*," Bibi would say with a soft smile. *Keep a cool heart.* It never paid to give in to the torrent. When all your life is on a stage, even a stage with bars, you learn quickly to cover your true emotions with a mask of convention. If all is not as it should be, at least it can appear that way.

And yet.

The rage I feel boiling inside me as I look up at Kiet is like water pushing to break through a dam, pushing with such force and power that I know I will not be able to hold it back. Maybe it's the brooding silences of the last few days. Maybe it's the many emotions all around me, felt but never shared. But mostly I think this is about starting down my own path of choice only to feel that power taken out of my hands yet again. By someone I'd thought I could trust.

How could Kiet betray me like this? How could he lie to my face?

I swallow hard and try to keep my voice level.

"The road out of here. Why did you say it is closed? It is open—open! I heard it from some travelers in the forest. Why?" My voice rises to a high squeak by the last word, and my face is burning.

Kiet's cheeks pale. "Luchi—I . . . you . . . I just thought you needed to stay here a while." He looks at me, his eyes soft and begging. "They are good people. It is a big change for you, going out in the world. I thought you needed—"

"You *thought*?" The words fly out of my mouth like stones. "What about me? Don't I get to think about things? Don't I get to choose?"

The flow of rage is not slowing. I thought releasing it would burn up all the anger, let me regain control. But it feels like the opposite is happening. Now the dam has broken and my current is a roar of white water, tugging me along and threatening to drag me under. The only thing I can do is keep moving.

I push past Kiet into the empty kitchen and then through to the sleeping room. On the far wall, my tea box and Mama's urn are piled on top of the folded sarong. I snatch them up and turn to leave when I see Yai sitting on the floor, legs tucked under her, hands folded in her lap. Her eyes are cast down and her face is twisted into a look that I cannot read, do not want to read. I know she must have heard our exchange on the porch. My shouted words.

If she has heard, others will have, too. Any concerns they might have had about my upbringing will be justified. They will be glad they kept Pensri away from me.

Swallowing hard, I remove the borrowed hat and lay it down in front of her. I lower myself into a *wai*. The traditional gesture, the pressing of palms and lowering of head, calms me a fraction. But as I open my mouth to explain, my heart starts to pound again. "I wish to say farewell, Khun Yai. I have learned that the roads are clear. I must now be on my way."

Yai only nods, and her eyes shine with understanding and maybe sorrow, too. "May the spirits of your ancestors go with you, child," she says. "It has been a good thing to have you at our table." And I know she does understand, and feel, and care.

I swallow, because in spite of my anger, in spite of the tension of the past days, in spite of Kiet, I do agree with her words. And appearances must be kept up. "It has been an honor to share your home," I say.

Then I turn and leave the room. Kiet is not in the kitchen, and I slip on my sandals and stride down the porch steps. Away.

I will make my own way. I don't need anyone else.

17

As I walk, the rain starts up again. I wrap my sarong tightly around my tea box, determined not to let in any moisture that might damage the precious contents.

It takes me less than fifteen minutes to get to the main road. I have heard the family talking about this road that leads back toward Sukhothai. From there, I will find a bus to take me to Bangkok. I have Isra's *baht*, so I will have no trouble paying my way.

The quiet afternoon air and the light rain lull me with their peace, and I think about my exchange with Kiet. Was I right in what I said, what I did? I lost face, and more important, I caused Kiet to lose face. But what else could I have done? The pushing in my chest was not something that could be controlled. I truly believe it was something that needed to grow, a moth that had to push its way out of the cocoon so that it might someday learn to fly.

I replay the memory in my mind. I see myself standing on that porch, telling Kiet what I thought, deciding what I had to do. All on my own. Not forced by circumstances outside of my control, but acting alone—choosing—for the first time in my life.

No. It was not a mistake, and I would bear an ocean of rain and a river of mud and the solitude of all the lonesome treks in the world to gain the strength that came from that choice.

Still, the rain and the mud are a poor exchange for my lost friendship, and I would be a fool not to see what I have lost.

The road to Sukhothai is longer than I had expected. After an hour's walk, I have no idea how far I have come or how far there is still to go. My hair hangs around my face in dripping strands and my clothes stick to my body. The soles of my feet are made of sandpaper. How much longer can I go on like this?

The road is well traveled, and each time a car or truck passes I scoot up onto the bank, getting as far away from it as I can. Yet I look wistfully after the clouds of exhaust, picturing wide-open doors and invitations to ride—anything, *anything* if I could just stop walking.

A pickup truck slows as it passes me, the paunchy driver in mirrored sunglasses swiveling his head around to study me as he goes by. Round lumpy figures line the back of the truck like a half-filled fruit bowl. I turn my head away from the man's buglike stare.

The truck drives only a few hundred meters, then stops and veers onto the side of the road in front of me. Suddenly I feel very exposed on this busy highway. My earlier wish for someone to stop seems reckless; this driver does not look like he has good intentions. I clutch my bundle closer to my chest and slow my walk.

The engine turns off.

My steps slow to an ant's crawl, but the truck waits. I have to reach it eventually. The shapes in the back unfold themselves into people, young girls and boys, with tight faces and empty eyes. I shudder, tearing my eyes away, breathing deeply as I come level with the driver's door.

The man leans out the window and moves his head to look me up and down. He drawls out a few words in what I can tell are a variety of languages. Then he croaks in English, "American?" He must see the flash of under-standing in my eyes because he lunges on. "All alone walk? You ride? Back on, get. You. No walk. Come!" He flashes what might be a dazzling smile except it is shot through with a terrible leer like I have seen only in the worst of late-night television.

I try not to tremble as I move past the front of the truck and away.

But not away. The engine starts up again and the truck idles along beside me, matching its pace to mine, the driver wheedling and cajoling, calling out promises and pleas. From the edge of my vision I can see the faces in the back drinking me in, studying me as if trying to guess what I will do.

Are they prisoners, or have they chosen their fate— whatever it is—willingly? If this man has a mind to take me by force, I would not be able to resist. Perhaps it would be better for me if I went willingly. And for a moment, with my feet aching and my skin dripping rain, the thought of a seat in that truck, any truck, feels like a chance worth taking. I could ride to Sukhothai, then find some way to escape.

My step falters and the truck pauses in response, the engine purring its encouragement.

And then I hear a voice from the back—a whisper so slight I almost miss it. But it cuts through the noise of the traffic and goes straight to my core. *"Jai Klaasi,"* the voice says. Keep your courage. Go forward bravely.

I take another breath, gasp at what I nearly allowed to happen. I have heard the stories told in the cells at night, about young girls lured away to unspeakable fates, held against their will, unable to escape. This is the truth: if I climb in that truck, I will not be able to get out in Sukhothai. But I *do* have a choice, right here and now, and I choose to go forward as best I can. I will be nobody's prisoner.

My eyes turn back to the road and I begin walking again, more quickly this time, determined. The driver must see my new stride, for he shouts out something I don't hear, and a form detaches itself from the glom of people in back. A tall, broad-shouldered man jumps over the side of the pickup and starts toward me.

He holds a syringe in his outstretched hand.

I don't need prompting to know what will happen if I don't get out of here. I break into a run.

But how can I escape? The truck is just meters behind me, and I am no match for this long-legged runner. Half turning to look over my shoulder, I see he is almost within arm's reach. What can I do?

Again the whisper sounds in my mind: Keep courage. Be strong.

There's a swish in the air behind me as the man grabs for my hair. He misses, but barely, and I feel a few strands pull loose from my scalp as he yanks at them.

Take it, I think. Pull it all out, but let me go free.

I will not give up. I cannot think like a *farang* right now, some foreigner in a *thoratat* movie who will run screaming until the killer plunges a knife into her back. No, I must use the wiles I have learned on the inside.

I must do the unexpected.

Quick as a raindrop, I throw my body to the side. I dash off the bank and run straight out into the middle of the road. I don't look behind me. I don't look to the side. I hear a loud *HOOOOONK* and feel the hot breath of a car that has just missed hitting me. I hear the angry roar of the pickup truck and know the driver must be trying to follow. I don't hear the footsteps of my pursuer, but I know they cannot be far behind.

I hold my tea box and steady Mama's urn on my back and run. I run like I have never run before. Straight across the highway, across the grassy middle, through the other lane of traffic—no cars coming this time, I thank my ancestors. And then on the other side, with the cars heading in the opposite direction, I keep running, fast and hard, moving with a desperate need for survival.

On and on and on.

What finally makes me stop is the iron hand squeezing my chest. I'm not used to this kind of exertion. My skin is pouring sweat, so that now I am soaked from the inside and out. My whole body shakes like I have the coughing fever. But when I drop to the ground and look back the way I've come, there is no one.

The pickup truck is gone. The man with the syringe no longer chases me. I am alone.

I am safe.

Exhilaration and relief and delayed terror course through me like an electric shock. I lean forward and wrap trembling arms around my legs, rocking myself back and forth, back and forth.

I don't know how long I stay like this. I only know that I never want to move again.

And then I hear the motor, a rattling clang that can be made by only one engine in the world.

I close my eyes in relief.

Kiet has come for me.

18

His car pulls onto the side of the road just ahead, and what a difference this vehicle is from the last one that stopped! Pulling myself together, I stand and move toward it on shaky legs. I pause only a second before the door. My anger at Kiet is not gone, but it feels small when placed against the danger of this outside world, at what I have just been through.

And while I have saved myself this time, I know I might not be so lucky the next. This road is no place for a girl on her own. I need Kiet.

Pulling on the door handle, I slide inside.

"I was looking for you," he says, voice dry and clipped. "I drove toward Bangkok. I did not expect you to be traveling backward."

"I thought to take a bus from Sukhothai. And then . . ." I swallow. "I had a little trouble."

He looks at me quickly, a flash of alarm in his eyes.

"It's all right. I got away. That's why I crossed over to this side of the highway. I was going to keep walking . . ."

My words seem useless, empty. They don't matter any-more. They don't even seem real.

Kiet must see that in my eyes because he nods and turns back to the road. We ride in silence for a while, but it's not the comfortable silence of friends. This air is thick with unspoken words, prickly with things unsaid.

He lied to me. He betrayed my trust.

But he also came for me. In spite of my outburst, and though I shamed him in front of his family. Is there some way we can put all this behind us, start things over?

We are picking up speed, puddles sloshing around us, the hum of rain pattering across the front window. Kiet reaches down and shifts the car into a higher gear. His jaw is tight, his fingers clamped around the gearshift.

Jai yen. Keep a cool heart. I can put this behind me; I can take this step. But I will do it in my own way. And so I reach out my right hand and place it on top of his.

Kiet freezes. I know it's not polite to be too affectionate in our culture, his culture—especially for a soon-to-be monk—but I want so much for him to understand me. I am a child of Thailand, I want to say, but I am also my own per-son. I am also someone else, from some far-off wild country, mysterious, unknown. A country with different shades of skin and different tones of language. A country where feel-ings do not always flutter within the chest but sometimes claw their way out into the open. I am not proud of all these things, but it is who I am.

In spite of everything, I want to tell him, I am

becoming who I am. All the bars in the world cannot keep me closed in now that I am free.

And more: I understand why he did what he did. I don't agree, and it was wrong, all wrong, but I know why he did it. And I understand and almost—almost—I am grateful.

I can't explain these things, can't even try to form the words, but I think them. And I don't know how much of my thoughts reach Kiet, but after a minute his grip under mine relaxes.

I study his face and when I see a smile crack the corner of his mouth, I let out a breath. He understands, then. The relief makes me giddy. Then I look down at myself, clothes dripping wet, half-covered in mud from the side of the road. And suddenly a laugh starts in my belly, creeping up my chest and rippling out until it's swallowing me up.

Kiet jumps at the sound. "What?" he says.

"Every time we go driving," I gasp out, still shaking with laughter, "I bring the monsoon into your car."

Suddenly this is the funniest thought I've ever had, and I just want to laugh and laugh and keep on laughing. And soon Kiet is laughing, too, his mouth open wide and his head tilted back so I'm not sure how he's even watching the road. And as we laugh, all the anger and uncertainty and fear, and everything I've gone through in the last few hours slips away and falls behind me, like the puddles by the side of the road, like something that's in the past, like this really is the road to my new life.

19

Now that the air is clear between us and we are back on our way to Bangkok, I have time to give careful thought to what is up ahead. Kiet is lighthearted and cracks jokes to try to make me smile. But I realize now that my outburst of hilarity was more about shock and relief than real humor. I try to play along with Kiet, but the laughter keeps getting stuck in my throat.

Every time I look out at the side of the road, I see the flash of the syringe, the stranger's big hands as he lunged for my neck.

I shake off the past and try, as the hours creep by, to focus on the future. For that is problem enough on its own.

Kiet must finally come to this same realization. "Luchi, tell me about your plans. What is up ahead for you?" He juts his chin in the direction of the gray mass in the far distance: Bangkok, *Krungthep Mahanakhon*, the City of Angels.

I told the chief warden of my plan to locate Mama's friends in Bangkok, and I told the same to Kiet when he asked me at the start of our journey. But in truth, my focus then was on gathering my strength to leave the prison. I had so little concept of the outside world that planning seemed impossible. Now I see that I am terribly unprepared: if my plan were a piece of art, it would be a stick figure. There is little more to it than skin and bone.

Kiet turns to look at me, then jerks the wheel to the side to avoid another car. "You do have a plan?" he asks. He does not seem as sure as he did a minute ago. He is also no longer laughing.

"I have those addresses and phone numbers," I say. "People my mother knew in Bangkok. I will go and talk to them, find out what they know. They can give me advice on how I will get to America."

Kiet's foot slams on the brake. He whips the steering wheel to the side and barrels up onto the shoulder of the road. A green pickup truck leans hard on the horn as it passes us by, sending a spray of mud down the side of Kiet's window. The driver is still cursing in the distance as Kiet looks at me with round eyes.

"*That* is your plan?" he says. "That's all of it? You are going to Bangkok to talk to someone you have never met, and you just expect them to help you?"

I try to make my voice strong, but I feel my insides tightening up. "Mama knew more than one person in Bangkok. There will be people who know how to reach my relations in America."

Kiet lowers his forehead onto the steering wheel and mutters under his breath. After a minute he digs into his back pocket and pulls out a mobile phone. "Here," he says. "Get out your phone numbers and start calling. You cannot just come to somebody's front door without announcing yourself. Tell them who you are and see if they are willing to help you, before you go all the way there."

I look at the tiny phone. It is not too different from the intercom system I used to play with on the inside. I can do this.

Setting the device in my lap, I bend over to open the lid of the tea box, focusing my full attention on it so I don't have to look at Kiet. But he is on the road again, back to avoiding potholes and dodging mud puddles. He, too, is making himself busy so he does not have to look in my direction.

I pull out the worn sheet of paper and hold it for a moment between my palms. The top is titled "Bangkok: Contacts" in blue ink. I look at the first name and number, take a deep breath, and open Kiet's mobile phone.

With trembling fingers, I begin to press the keys.

20

It's after the third call that I realize this may not work as I had intended. How long ago were these numbers written? More than thirteen years, certainly; from before Mama went inside. The first two numbers I call are disconnected, and the third is answered by a brash, loud woman who has never heard of the name I ask for. Two more numbers, with no better result. Looking at it closely now, I wonder if the handwriting is my mother's after all. Is it possible someone else—my father, maybe—wrote these down? Do I have any chance of making a connection? With every incomplete call, Kiet's eyebrows sink lower down over his eyes, and I know I will have to think of something.

Soon there is only one left. The line buzzes and a mechanized voice tells me that the number I am calling no longer exists. What now?

If I tell Kiet that I have no more leads, he will feel obligated to take care of me. He will want to fix things and make them go according to a plan of his own making.

I have forgiven him for his well-meant control, but I haven't forgotten. This is *my* problem. I have to make my own solution. Things worked out with my escape from the men in the pickup truck; surely I can handle this, too.

All I need is to form another plan. A better one.

I shift in my seat and feel a crinkling in my pocket. The paper Jeanne gave me, the letter from my grandmother. Relief washes over me like a wave. *Regina Finn. 21 Stafford Circle. Brookline, Massachusetts, USA.*

There is my plan: This address will take me just where I need to go. I can make my way to Bangkok, and from there I can complete this journey on my own.

And so I take a deep breath, and once again pull my future into my own hands. It feels easier this time, but I am no less terrified.

My fingers are steady now as I dial again: this time, a random string of numbers that will call up nothing at all. The mobile is warm in my palm and I shift it to my left hand, away from Kiet so he will not hear that there is no voice on the other end.

"Hello?" I make my voice bright, casual. "Yes—oh good, this is just who I was hoping to speak with." I do not stumble as I speak all the proper Thai honorifics. Kiet will have no doubt that I am speaking to Thakoon Ngakom, eminent Bangkok lawyer and philanthropist. I launch into a description of my mother, pause for several imagined responses, and finally decide that I can take no more. I call an abrupt end to the conversation.

Closing the phone with a final sigh, I turn to Kiet. "He will see me the day after tomorrow," I say. "He was very busy and could not talk long. But he remembers my mother. He can connect me with my relatives in America. He can help me to travel there."

Kiet looks like a tire that has just been refilled with air. His shoulders relax and his mouth spreads into a wide smile. "That is good news," he says, and his grin is contagious.

There was no news, good or otherwise, so why do I suddenly feel so relieved? Am I just giddy with the feeling of guiding my own destiny? Or maybe it is the comfort of sitting here, with a friend, in a car filled with warmth and music, where I can see the stormy gray skies and the gushing rain all around but know that, for this moment at least, there is no way they can touch me.

PART II

Deliverance

21

The road grows wider now that we are approaching the city. There are three fat lanes, all jammed with cars going in the same direction as us. Through a mass of bushes and trees I can see more rows of cars and trucks on the opposite side, heading back the way we came. We are packed on this street as tightly as prisoners in a cell, but instead of familiarity and comfort I just feel small.

I squeeze my hands into fists. The fear that churns suddenly in my belly makes me remember one mealtime, as a very young child, when I became separated from Mama in the dining area. I turned around and she was gone, and suddenly the cafeteria was a blur of bodies, hair, and hands and faces that suddenly looked the same and I was alone, all alone—

"Luchi?"

I catch myself, coming out of my remembering with a gasp. It takes two or three shakes to clear my head, but I smile weakly at Kiet. "I am all right. I was only thinking—" I frown at the gridlock of vehicles, at the clouds of black smoke boxing us in on all sides, at the miserable weeping sky that makes me want to cry, too. I swallow hard. "Never mind. This is just so different from everything I've grown up with. So far from the inside."

Kiet looks at me, and his eyes smile out kindness and understanding. He is a small-town boy, I remember. He knows what it's like to come to the big city for the first time.

"Just wait," he says now. "We are almost in Bangkok. I want you to do something for me."

We drive on a ways farther, and then Kiet tells me to close my eyes. He turns on the radio again, and suddenly the car is filled with a rich clatter of sounds—cymbals and drums and a loud waterfall of piano keys. It is big and loud and alive, and then— "Look, now. Open your eyes!"

And I do.

We are in Bangkok, the City of Angels.

My mouth falls open. Nothing I have seen on paper or television comes close to the majesty of this place. I know we aren't yet near the downtown center, the city's heart, but still the size of everything pulls at my eyes, tugging them this way and that. I follow the lines of the buildings up, up, and feel that I too could touch the sky, if only I would stretch my hand out far enough.

What magic is this that Kiet has worked for me? We are still crammed onto a street packed with cars, swirled in fumes, but now the music sets the tone, and the beat rings out joy and wonder.

Kiet is lost in his own thoughts also, and I am glad. This gives me time to hear the city's drumbeat inside my heart. The bigness all around makes me think of my own destiny. Do I have a plan that touches the sky?

Do I have a plan at all?

"I have been thinking more about how I will travel to America," I say abruptly.

Kiet turns to look at me. "What have you decided?" he asks, reaching over to lower the music.

This is a good question, and one for which I have no full answer. But I do have an idea. I reach inside the tea box and pull out the tiny cloth purse stuffed with Mama's American dollars. I don't know exactly how American money works, but the stack is thick and seems to hold a lot of zeroes.

I show the bag to Kiet. I say, "Here. This is how I will get where I need to go." I tilt my head and look at him, suddenly unsure. "Do you think this will work? Will it be enough?"

He peers into the bag and his eyebrows rise. "Yes, I think that will do well." He pauses a moment, then says, "The lawyer. He will know the best way to travel. This money will see you safely there. But he will advise you."

My heart sinks. Yes, the lawyer friend of my mother's would surely have some excellent advice for me. If only he existed. If only one of the numbers in the book was still active, if it belonged to a person who still remembered one American woman from so long ago.

I also know that if I spoke to the right person, I could probably find a way to contact my grandmother, this stranger of my own blood who was so concerned for my mother. I have heard there is an American embassy, right here in Bangkok. Surely they would know what to do. But just thinking of this possibility makes a sweat break out on my forehead. It is too hostile. Too unknown.

Mama's dire warnings, her cautions that I never reveal myself to outsiders, still ring loud in my mind even after all this time. What about the terror that dogged her every waking moment? Can I so easily ignore it, without knowing what it was? No. I am not ready to break the silence of a lifetime. There is still too much of my mother in me.

And what about her last words, her dying wish? She charged me to keep her secrets, and so I can only see one path before me now. I must learn everything. I must discover those secrets for myself. Only then will I know who to trust, how to act, who to be.

The song on the radio ends, and a woman starts to chirp out some peppy dialogue. Kiet turns it off, and Bangkok is once again just a city.

A city with ways and paths and secrets that can be discovered. And somewhere, the clues to the mystery that lies at the core of my life.

22

All day I've worried about how I will get Kiet to leave me in Bangkok. I know that he feels responsible for my care, yet I also know that I cannot be the new person I need to be, so long as he is looking over my shoulder. I think back to those hikers I met in the woods, the way they looked at me—just like I was an ordinary girl. They didn't see the bars of my childhood.

I want to be that girl again, that easy-life person with no secret past. But I can't do that with Kiet beside me. I need to go out on my own. Of course, this will bring its own problems; I haven't forgotten the danger on the road to Sukhothai. But the more time passes, the more confident I feel.

If only I could persuade Kiet that I will be all right, that he can leave me and move on to his place at the temple. But how can I possibly do that?

Kiet himself solves my problem with a frown that grows and grows over the course of an hour, until finally he says: "I am supposed to be at the *wat* by four o'clock tomorrow morning. It is far south of Bangkok; with traffic it will take me hours to reach. I don't know what to do—if we stayed longer with my family I had planned to officially register a delay, but now that I am so close . . ."

He trails off, the strings of responsibility tugging him in different directions, leaving him tied and powerless. From the look on his face, I can see how much his place at the temple means to him, and I marvel that he would have delayed it for my sake.

I also send a thankful nod to providence, which has given me an easy escape. "Kiet, it will be all right. You were supposed to drive me to Bangkok, not care for me the rest of my life."

He laughs at this, then frowns again. "Bangkok is a big city. It is not at all safe for a young girl alone, a *farang*."

"I am not a foreigner," I say. "You know I was born near Chiang Mai."

Kiet shoots me a glance that pierces me right through, and I understand his meaning. I am not just a *farang* in Thailand; I am a *farang* in this world, this wide new life of freedom.

But I shake my head. "I will manage," I say. "I can find somewhere to stay until it is time to meet with the lawyer." This man has become so real, I almost believe in him myself. But Kiet has something else in mind.

"I have a friend I can introduce you to," he says. "For many years I drove a motorcycle taxi on Sukhumvit Soi 2. I know someone there who will take care of you. She will help you to get where you need to go."

My heart sinks at the thought of someone else to watch me. Yet how can I refuse Kiet? And as I think on it more, a friend with a motorcycle could be useful. I don't know Bangkok, and I will need to save my money to be able to travel. The *baht* that Isra gave me cannot last very long.

And, of course, what that really means is just one thing. Soon, I tell myself. I must find my path soon.

23

By the time we arrive downtown, the gray sky of day has changed to the grayer sky of early night. The long hours of city traffic have flown by. Everywhere I turn, there is so much to see. Even the rain that gushes down in torrents does not dampen my enthusiasm. Everything in the world is bright, streaked with reflected light and color, and to me it looks clean and scrubbed and new.

I am seeing it for the first time, and it is putting on its best face for my benefit.

All along the streets are buildings and shops with colorful signs and garish advertisements. People jostle along the sidewalks, sheltered under umbrellas or raincoats or sometimes open magazines, moving from one place to another with a casual determination, with smiles and laughter. I myself cannot stop smiling at all the life I see pushing around me, as I sit safely behind my glass walls and look and look.

On Sukhumvit Road we stop at a big, brightly lit store called 7-Eleven, though I am not sure why those numbers are important. Inside it is full of white light, and Kiet buys me a bowl of prawn dumplings that are heated up inside a microwave. Kiet murmurs in my ear, explaining how a store works. He pulls out money and hands it to the woman at the cash register, counts the coins that are given back, and finally nods. We take our dumplings and our water bottles and return to the car. The food is hot and filling, although it came from a package and makes me long for the meals that Kiet's family prepared.

It is nearly full dark by the time we turn onto Sukhumvit Soi 2. I look at the plastic watch on my wrist and see that it is a little after six o'clock. Kiet pulls his car halfway onto the sidewalk and turns off the engine. Reaching over into the backseat, he grabs a gray-green satchel and hands it to me.

"This is for you," he says. "I put a few things inside—things you will need on your journey. You can put your other items in here as well."

I cannot think of any words to say. The car is suddenly very loud, exploding with the sound of the rain on the roof. I pull open the drawstrings of the bag and look inside. There are a few familiar items—a brush, soap, some food items, and . . . I pull out the square of silk and a small bundle of colored thread. The needlepiece I was working on with Yai. I touch the tangle of brown and green thread and my eyes fill with tears.

"Kiet," I say.

But he is brisk now, trying to fill the awkward parting

with necessary business. He scribbles on a piece of paper and hands it to me. "My mobile phone number," he says, "and my e-mail address. If you can find your way to a computer. I don't know how much contact I will have once I am initiated, but I want to remain in touch. Perhaps one day—" He shrugs and smiles. "Who knows what the future will bring?"

I take his paper and put it into my pocket. I have only known this new Kiet a few days, so why do I feel as though losing him will cost me a portion of my heart?

"Thank you," I whisper. I tilt my head and look up at him—the first, the only boy I have ever known. And there is nothing more I can add nor any way to say it better. So I just say it again: "Thank you."

We climb out of the car, and I move forward on heavy stone feet.

Through the pouring rain I can see the *motosai* drivers, lined up next to their motorbikes with their bright orange jackets. The bikes are clustered under an overhang that gives them next to nothing in the way of shelter. All the drivers are soaked through.

As we wait, a young woman in a short skirt and heels walks up to the lead bike. She exchanges words with the driver and hops onto the back, sitting with both legs to one side, feet neatly crossed at her ankles. The driver revs the motor and squeals off into the traffic. My mouth drops open as the bike skims around the side of a white pickup truck, darts in front of a bus, and disappears around a corner.

Kiet grins. "There are days when I miss the *motosai rap jang*. Those wild rides!"

I must look worried—and I am, because this crazy riding seems more cause for alarm than longing.

But Kiet laughs at me and waves toward the group gathered by the bikes. "Chaluay!" he calls. One of the drivers looks up with a smile for Kiet, and I have time to observe her as she strides toward us. A bit of a novelty on Soi 2, Kiet tells me, Chaluay is one of the few female *motosai* drivers. She is young, and I don't see much to tell her apart from the male drivers. Maybe just a certain slant to her chin and a careful way she walks. But her hair is cut short and her look is hard. She holds her hands like they might be ready to grip a hammer. A girl who has grown up in a man's world. She looks to me like someone who has had to fight for every step she took.

"Kiet," Chaluay says, coming close enough to be heard through the rain. They exchange *wais* and I follow suit, lowering myself below both of their levels to show my inferior status.

"You look well," he says to her, and grins.

"Who is this *farang*?" she asks. Her own smile fades as she looks at me, the foreigner. "Did you bring me a rider? You know I can't take anyone out of turn." She waves toward the line of drivers, each waiting for the next customer to arrive.

"No, nothing like that." Kiet suddenly looks uncomfortable, as if he only just realized that his plan might be less simple than he'd thought. "This is Luchi. She is a friend of mine—and she will be leaving Bangkok soon. But she needs somewhere to stay for a few days, and I was hoping that you might . . ." He trails off, perhaps seeing the look on Chaluay's face. I recognize that look, worn frequently by women on the inside when someone was moving in on their space or trying to take one of their privileges.

Deciding to give them some time alone, I mutter an excuse and sidle away. I walk along the row of motorbikes, watch the traffic, count the raindrops as they tap-dance on the inky puddles around me. Nearly fifteen minutes go by before I hear the sound of slapping feet behind me and I turn to find Kiet, dripping wet and smiling.

He has a great smile, I think to myself.

I don't know what Kiet has said to Chaluay, but when I return she behaves something very close to friendly. She apologizes for her first reaction, and I quickly cut short her explanation—after all, I am the houseguest who has fallen from the sky.

So I just lower my head and thank her and then she is saying good-bye to Kiet and I turn and all the rain running down my face cannot mask the wet of my eyes. I know he sees the sadness welling up inside me, and what is more, I think he feels a bit of it, too.

Because when I look in his eyes for the last time, I suddenly remember how he tried to delay this moment. How he tried to have us stay a little longer in that old teak house in the mountains. And whether my soul needed the growing or only my heart, I am suddenly thankful for that gift of extra time.

But I will miss him.

24

Even after Kiet drives away and his car fades to a dull rainy speck, I keep my eyes fixed on that distant nothing. This is only partly because of Kiet. The main reason is that I can't think what to say to the brooding stranger standing beside me.

But a minute later, Chaluay turns and begins to walk away fast, heading toward the line of motorbikes. "*Pai*," she calls over her shoulder, as though just now deciding that I should come with her. "I would have finished work in another hour anyway. I might as well leave now."

I shift my sack to a more comfortable spot on my shoulder and scramble after her. By the time I catch up, she has spoken to some of the other drivers, all of whom are looking at me curiously.

"Here's a helmet," Chaluay says, and tosses me a hard round hat, which I've seen the other riders put on before they drive away. But Isra wore no such thing on her bicycle rides.

My helmet is yellow and has a pull-down plastic

window on the front. Chaluay slides a black one over her own head and tucks her hair down inside her collar.

"Thank you." I copy her movements, and feel like I am putting my head inside a tiny car. It doesn't make me feel safer, though. She climbs on her bike and I turn my body sideways to sit on the back, as I saw the young woman do a few minutes ago, but Chaluay stops me.

"You should straddle the seat. You are wearing shorts and the rain will make the roads slippery." She pulls out a small smile. "It is safer that way."

At the front of the line of bikes, a man in a crumpled suit is climbing on behind another driver. The man's legs are splayed out to each side. He clings to his driver's waist, but even so he nearly falls back onto the pavement as the *motosai* skids off onto the main road. I nod; this was how I rode on Isra's bicycle. Only without the rain, or the screeching traffic, or the dark helmet swallowing my entire head.

Riding on Chaluay's bike will definitely take some learning. If Kiet were the one driving, I might ask about speeds and corners and what is the safest way to hold on. But this is not Kiet, and I am uncomfortable enough as it is.

When Chaluay kicks her engine to life, I don't make a sound. But my hands, in their death grip on her waist, are screaming. I see right away how this ride is going to be: all rumble and roar and clouds of choking black smoke.

I squeeze my eyes shut and breathe slowly in and out.

If I had not seen the other drivers, I would think that

Chaluay is trying to frighten me. Instead, I realize that she is probably being especially careful. But I do not want to see that vehicle I can feel whizzing by my knee. I pull my legs in closer and bite down hard on my bottom lip.

I have to get used to this. It is just another way of the world, this new world that I am now a part of. All I need to do is sit on this *motosai* and not open my mouth. It is just like being on Isra's bicycle, only faster. And louder. And far crazier.

All right, it is nothing like Isra's ride, but I *must* put up with it.

If I want to be a real part of this real world, I have to make myself take these steps, no matter how terrified I am.

Slowly, I open my eyes.

And in spite of myself, I gasp. The world around me is black, flecked with spots of bright color that flash by like stars in my own personal universe. We are going faster than the rain, and it swooshes around me like a wide, wet sheet. Without the darkness of my closed eyes to tear the movements into random jerks, I see a pattern to our travel. A turn here, a sharp corner there.

We are going so fast that all my worries, all my fears and indecisions are torn away behind me.

And then a realization rolls over me, like a rush of madness, and I let out one loud whoop of delight: I *do* love this moment, this ride, this rain, this dark—this whole crazy world I have been thrust into.

It terrifies me, but oh, how I love the living of it!

25

Chaluay lives in one of those high-rise slap-together buildings that you always see in the news pieces about the Bangkok slums. We climb eight flights of stairs and she throws open her door with as much pride as if she's showing me the local *wat*. It's no temple, but the size of it takes my breath away—I could fit five of my old cots, end to end, along the far wall! All this living space for one person? The apartment is one big room, with a cooking area to the side and a door on the far end that must lead to a bathroom. Plastic wrappers dot the floor, lending splashes of color to the dull gray linoleum. I am starting to appreciate Chaluay's taste already. Then my eyes find the couch, which lies half-buried in rumpled clothes. My mouth gapes open. At a quick glance I can see three or four pairs of jeans, and the bright colors of at least six shirts and dresses. What could Chaluay possibly do with all those clothes? I consider this rough-edged girl, not many years older than me, with renewed respect. Everything in this apartment belongs to her. Even the sour air must smell sweet to Chaluay, because it is home and it is all her own.

It is a staggering thought. Surely no *wat* could be more precious than this.

Chaluay throws her helmet on the floor and peels off her wet jacket. She kicks aside some of the clothes and rolls out a lumpy sleeping mat for me while I go into the bathroom to change. In the tiny room alone, I hold Yai's sarong to my cheek and smile, grateful that I can take off my wet, muddy clothes. I wash them out in the sink and hang them to dry. Unlike Chaluay, I will need to use them again tomorrow. I may not have nearly as much, but every item I own is a treasure.

Our evening passes slowly, uncomfortably. Chaluay is nothing like Kiet. She will help me because she was asked to, but she obviously finds no joy in it. I am a duty she will tend to, nothing more. We eat some instant noodles and I am glad when we turn out the lights and I lay down on my mat.

In the dark, I tuck my arms behind my head and study what I can see of the ceiling. Chaluay's breathing slows to a measured tread, and I think of Mama. I remember a long-ago night when I was still very young, a night like so many others. The guards had settled down for the late watch, Bibi was snoring on her bunk, and Jeanne too was finding her peace in dreams. I was on my cot, listening until the time was right.

There was a certain magic moment, when the quiet

was just perfect—a breath, a snore, a sigh from outside the bars. Then I crawled out of bed and slipped in next to Mama. She was curled up tight in the blanket, trying to hold her warmth against the damp night air. But she saw me come and flipped down the edge of her covers, scooted over to make room.

I made myself into a ball and slid into the space her body made for me. We lay side by side, breathing in the quiet. Then Mama whispered, "You have to go to sleep, baby. You know the tooth fairy won't come until you're asleep."

My tooth had gone under the pillow earlier that night, but this was not my first lost tooth. I knew who was really the one leaving a treat for me to find in the morning. Still, I liked to play along.

"How can the tooth fairy find us in here?" I asked. The words tickled the empty space at the front of my mouth and I giggled.

"She will find us; she always does," said Mama. And then her voice got very quiet and faraway. "But nobody else will. We are safe here, and that's what matters."

The tremor in her voice made me wriggle closer and reach back to pull her hand over my shoulder like a shawl. I *was* safe, and warm, and happy. And in the morning there would be a wrapped candy under my pillow, and Isra had promised to take me to the market on the weekend.

I had everything I wanted in the world.

I slept.

26

The next morning when I come out of the washroom dressed in my clean—though still-damp—clothes, Chaluay greets me with a tentative smile.

"I must apologize for yesterday. I behaved poorly. I . . ." She seems to be searching for reasons but not finding them, so I cut her off quickly.

"No, I am the one who needs to apologize for arriving without warning. You are very kind to let me stay with you."

Chaluay waves that away. Her smile is real, I think, though her mouth is still stretched a little tight. She is obviously trying very hard to be friendly. "Kiet said you were born up-country and have lived there your whole life."

I had wondered what Kiet told her about my past. But something in the way she says this—curious but not alarmed, interested but not desperate to know—tells me that he said nothing about Khon Mueang Women's Prison. Did he guess at my wish to start anew? I smile. I really *can* be anybody I want to, now.

I will tell Chaluay nothing more than I must.

"Yes, up-country," I say. "North of Chiang Mai."

"And your parents?" she prompts.

"My mother has recently died. I am now returning to America to . . . be with my father. And other relatives." I am once again surprised at how normal these careful slivers of fact make me sound.

Chaluay never even blinks. She moves right on to the next subject. "This cannot be your first time in Bangkok!" When I nod that it is, she claps her hands together. "Today, I do not need to start my shift until after midday. Would you like to go downtown? There is so much for you to see—Bangkok is the greatest city in the world!"

Her enthusiasm is contagious. For the first time I feel I might find a friend in this strange, moody girl. "Yes," I say. "I would like that very much."

Chaluay studies me approvingly. "You are not like other *farang*. If I was not looking at you, if I only heard you speak, I would think you were Thai."

A cold fist clenches in my stomach. My familiarity with the Thai language could easily bring up questions that I have no wish to answer. I need to move away from that subject as quickly as possible. "Well, I have done much traveling," I say, letting the eager smile slide off my face, trying to sound cool and world-weary. "But I feel a special connection with the Thai culture. I spent my whole life and . . . I studied here."

Chaluay shrugs, and that familiar scowl seems to flutter back between her brows. "Good for you. It must be nice to be able to travel so much." She gives herself a little shake, and her smile is back. "But never to have seen Bangkok! We must lose no time."

I stifle a sigh of relief as we move away from that shaky ground, and I follow Chaluay down the stairs. We step out the front door of her building, into the soft morning drizzle, and climb onto her bike, which she has left chained outside. Chaluay revs up the motor and we are off.

How much there is to see! The wind roars outside my helmet, but my mind replays over and over the majestic symphony music that Kiet chose for my entry into this magnificent City of Angels. All around me, everything is so big, so bright, so busy! The colors of my childhood were gray and dull brown, with the only bright splashes found in the green trees and the deep blue sky. Occasional festivals and market days were explosions of color that fed my soul for weeks.

But here—this whole city is a rainbow. Bright electric lights flash on the sides of buildings, even now that it's daytime. Shops are lined with colorful awnings, and women strut by dressed in hot pink and orange and yellow. In the public gardens and near tall fancy buildings, there are flowers—real, living flowers, with delicate purple and white petals. And the *wats*! Temples so tall and ornate that I feel holy just looking at their doors.

I could stop on every corner and stare for hours, but Chaluay keeps up a speedy pace, zipping down one street and on to the next. Cars are packed in tightly everywhere, but she slips in and around them with effortless skill so that, like a bird in flight, we never need to stop moving. Meanwhile she talks to me over her shoulder—keeps up a steady stream of friendly banter, introducing and explaining and advertising all in one. She is a wonder.

I crane my neck and try to understand the Skytrain, something I have not learned about in my encyclopedias. This train does not run on or below the ground, but on a track built high in the air, on special columns dotted across the city. We tour the wide green gardens of Dusit Park, view the temple grounds of the Wat Saket, and finally, as the sun rises higher in the dripping sky, we park the motorbike and climb more than three hundred steps to the top of the Golden Mount. Chaluay tells me with some pride, as though it was partly her doing, that until fifty years ago this was the highest spot in Bangkok. Now, of course, there are skyscrapers and many other structures taller than this.

But I look down from this height and am awed. The view is like nothing I have seen before—in fact, it *is* nothing I have seen before. To be this far above the ground— imagine! The city stretches out below me like a jeweled carpet, every rooftop a precious stone. I feel like the queen of a magnificent city.

"And this is just one city," I whisper. The idea feels strange to me, but for the first time I start to understand how truly big the world is. For one crazy moment I'm so filled with emotion that I want to grab Chaluay in a giant hug, the way I would Mama as a child. But I know I can't do that. I sneak a glance at Chaluay, who is also looking out over the city, and caution myself again to control my show of feelings. Play the part, I tell myself. Be normal.

"So, you are going to America soon." Chaluay's voice drags my thoughts back into focus.

"Yes," I whisper, though this is something I have been loath to think about. "Soon."

"You have family there?"

"Yes." That much has to be true, though I know of none of them except my grandmother. But Chaluay is waiting for more details. I try to think of what else I can add without being entirely untruthful. "Yes, many relatives. They are all . . . businessmen. They are very anxious to see me after so long." I cringe at how awkward my newborn story sounds. But I now see that Chaluay, staring off in the distance, seems to be lost in thoughts of her own.

"You will fly there, I suppose?" she says. My mouth drops open in confusion and she quickly adds, "On an airplane?"

I blush and nod. Of course. To cover my embarrassment I pat my bag. "My mother left me the money to travel. Soon I will need to go downtown to find out about airplanes that go to the United States."

Her eyes flick briefly to my bag and she shrugs. "I will show you something very special next," she says. "You cannot visit Bangkok without seeing the great river, Mae Nam Chao Phraya."

"River?" I echo. I know all about large bodies of water, of course. I've learned the names of the oceans and can recite the chemical composition of lake water. But none of those were ever real to me. They were blue blobs on an atlas page, nothing more. The tub in the bathing room back on the inside, that's the only pool of water I know. That was a busy room, full of noise and confusion. But the water itself was shallow and contained, a place to wash and clean and sometimes even play. The thought of being near running water as deep and dark and wide as my worst fears makes me feel like a child again, needing to curl up in my mother's arms. I can hardly imagine, in this moment, a thing I fear more.

I twist the strap on my wristwatch. "What time does your shift begin?" It is past eleven already.

Chaluay looks at her own watch and frowns. "It is later than I thought. The rain is getting harder, too. Well, let's get something to eat. You said you have things to do in town?"

I nod, and she turns to head back down the stairs. "That will take care of today. The river will just have to wait."

She smiles, but there is something crooked about it, like it has been sewn on and the stitching is starting to come ever so slightly loose. I put all the warmth I can into my own return smile. There was a seed of friendship trying to come out, I know there was. I hope Chaluay will give it a chance to grow.

I also hope that our time will be so full that she'll forget all about wanting to take me to the river.

27

Chaluay drops me off in Siam Square and leaves me there to walk up and down the streets, explore the shops, or do whatever I like with my afternoon. As her bike roars out of sight, my shoulders tighten. There is business to be done today. I must learn about airplane travel.

Straightening the strap of my pouch, I look around me. And then I gulp and nearly stumble.

For the first time since arriving in Bangkok, I am alone. People around me talk, laugh, push, jostle. They speak into small mobile phones and they squawk at their children. They look coyly at boys or girls near them. They move fluidly through this dance of life without giving it a second thought. And here I stand, stuck on the side with my dancing shoes still in hand. It is not that I don't know the right moves—I don't even hear the same music.

With a deep breath, I center my mind on what matters: learning about travel to America. One step at a time. I set to work exploring my surroundings, looking for clues that will point me to the right path.

But where to begin? Down the street as far as I can see, and on side streets in every direction, so many different shops clatter out a noisy jumble of objects: T-shirts with big cartoon faces of monkeys and frogs; radios pumping out music loud enough to make my teeth rattle as I walk by; televisions so thin and shiny I would watch them even if the screens were dark and empty; and everywhere, food and drinks and sweets of all types. All the bright colors promise so many new discoveries, but how can people take all this in at once? There are *things* everywhere—more than I could ever need, more than I can even imagine. It is simply too much. I fight a desire to cover my eyes and ears and retreat into a dark doorway, to seek out some small moment of quiet.

But I will myself to be strong. I push past the stalls and the awnings; I turn away from the flashing signs; I step out of the way of bustling shoppers with loud voices and over-flowing bags. Some of these people might know where to find what I am looking for, but it is beyond me to approach them and ask for help. It is all I can do to keep my eyes facing forward and to keep on moving. And with every new shop, in every new window I keep looking for the right sign.

I don't find it. But I do see something else. A neat store window, with no blinking lights or yelling merchants. The display is full of books. And one in particular catches my eye. As I step inside, a perky shopgirl eyes me hungrily, starts to chatter about sales and prices. But I shake my head.

"Please," I say, bringing my hands together in a *wai*. "I would just like to see that book in the window."

She nods and leans over to pull it out for me.

Cinderella.

My eyes fill as I run my fingers over the smooth binding, feel the crisp pages. It's not the same book I read nearly every day as a child. The pictures are different and there are no gold curlicues on the cover. But it's the same story, the story I know by heart. The poor orphaned girl who grows up to become a princess. Who finds her happily ever after.

It feels like a bit of home out here in this busy, smelly city. I pull out some of the *baht* Isra gave me and pay the shopgirl, as Kiet showed me in the 7-Eleven. And as I step back out into the street with the book tucked snugly into my bag, my head feels suddenly clear, my step strong, my mind focused.

I am here on a mission, and I won't stop until I find what I am seeking.

This thought sustains me while I walk up one street and down the next. And finally, when I'm starting to wonder if perhaps such a place doesn't exist at all, I see it. A tiny shop, squeezed in between two tall, gaudy buildings. The window, hardly wider than a rush mat, is bare except for a hand-lettered sign that says simply: TRAVEL.

At last.

I push through the door and a bell tinkles. Inside the shop, it's even hotter and more humid than it was out on the street. But what space there is has been transformed into a global paradise. Posters cover every wall, bright glossy images with captions like: EXPLORE ECUADOR! BALI IS A TROPICAL DREAM! And, most wonderfully: SEE AMERICA TODAY!

The America poster shows dry rugged mountains of reddish stone and smiling people wearing jeans and sunglasses. I slide over to it almost without realizing I've moved. I trace one finger along the border. Is this what Brookline, Massachusetts, looks like?

At a sound behind me I turn.

"Hello, young woman," says a man behind the counter. His flat nose makes him look like he's wearing a mask, but his eyes are kind. He speaks to me in English, and I smile at the way people assume I am a *farang*. And why shouldn't they?

I leave the poster and move to the counter, replying in Thai. "I would like some information about traveling to America."

He raises an eyebrow. "You are alone?"

"Yes."

He frowns, and his nose flattens even further. But he turns toward a gray computer, much like the one Chief Warden Kanya had in her office. "Where in America?" he asks me.

"I want to go to Brookline, Massachusetts." Saying the words out loud sends a tremor through me. It's a thrill of joy, of possibility, but also of sadness, because it's a part of Mama that she turned her back on, and I may never know why.

"Brookline?" says the man. Then, "Massachusetts. Boston?"

I think about this. Mama spent a full week teaching me all the American states and their capitals, but it was such a chore that I made no effort to remember them afterward. But those two names sound right together. "Yes," I say, then add: "I need to travel very soon. In a few days."

"You know that will be more expensive, yes? Do you have money to pay for this ticket?" His look is cautious, like he's not sure what to make of me, like he's trying to be nice but thinks deep down maybe I'm just playing a joke on him.

I pull my eyebrows together. Reaching into my bag, I grab the pouch containing my dollars. I push down a tickle of worry; of course there will be enough! Pulling open the zipper, I dump the stack of money out onto the counter. It falls into place with a soft *thump,* and out of the upside-down pouch, something else falls, too. A small key on a red plastic key ring.

Over at the computer, the man freezes in place. His nose twitches and he leans down, looking furtively from side to side as if he's afraid the walls might be spying on us. "Foolish girl, what do you think you're doing?" he snaps. He crams the bills back into the pouch, shutting the zipper with an angry hiss. "Do you know how much money you have here?"

My cheeks burn and I shake my head.

"A lot. Too much. You should not be carrying this money around and you certainly shouldn't be displaying it in public."

I know my lip is trembling, and he must see it too because his eyes soften. He presses the pouch into my hand. "Not everyone in this city will be honest and treat you well. You be very careful with that money. All right?"

I nod and stuff the pouch back into my bag.

"What's this?" he asks.

The little silver key is still on the counter. I pick it up and look carefully at the plastic keychain. There is a label with writing on it, faded and smudged but just barely visible: *BK Storage #391*

"You have left your luggage here? BK Storage?" It's a place he is apparently familiar with. And I have no idea what he is talking about. "They are good people—it is run by a foreigner, in fact. A little unconventional, but they provide a fine service. And they are honest. Do you know how to get back there?"

I shake my head, so he pulls out a sheet of notepaper and draws me a simple map with directions. Then he talks more about tickets and reservations and scheduling and asks me if I want to pay for my fare now and tells me how easy it is to take care of, right here with no difficulties. He talks and talks, but after a while I don't hear a word he says because my mind is raging and storming and shrieking with emotion, because—because—

There was a key in Mama's money bag. A key to a storage locker.

A key, maybe, to understanding my past.

How can I buy my ticket without first knowing what

secrets, what treasures, what information awaits me there? I might find something that turns my plans completely around, something that changes everything.

I thank the man for his time and tell him I cannot buy the ticket yet, tell him I will be back. Then, crushing my key tight in my hand, I push through the door and head back out into the rain.

After walking a few minutes, I finally slow my mind enough to think clearly and duck under an awning to study the scribbled map. BK Storage is on Rama IV, not too far from Siam Square, but it's getting dark now and the idea of exploring at night is too alarming. And what if I were late to meet Chaluay? I'm not certain she would wait for me, and I have no way to find her apartment alone.

I think for a moment how easy it would be for Chaluay to drive me to the storage place, if I had the courage to ask her. With her knowledge of the side streets and short cuts, we could probably be there in minutes.

I think of her smile, her eager look this morning. And again I think: she could become a friend. But this errand is part of my secret past. I cannot bring Chaluay here without telling her everything about myself.

And that is something I'm not willing to do.

No, this step is mine to take alone. I will not share it with her.

28

The rain pours down in sheets as I stand on the busy sidewalk, waiting for Chaluay. People push past me, cowering under bright umbrellas, under raincoats, under open newspapers or plastic shopping bags. But what do I care for rain? I, who have spent my life so sheltered, love this new way of knowing the elements. I smile and tilt my head back, close my eyes to the sky, and let the torrent do its worst.

It might be minutes or hours later, but finally Chaluay beeps her horn and I open my eyes and see her. I smile and she motions for me to come.

We ride back to her apartment in silence. I'm still lost in my day's discoveries, anticipating all that tomorrow might bring. As I crawl into my bed and drift off to sleep, I resolve that first thing in the morning I will ask Chaluay to drop me off near BK Storage. I will find my secret mystery.

But Chaluay has other plans.

I am woken in the still-dark of early morning, her

rough hands shaking me out of a dream of keys swirling in a cloud of black exhaust smoke, of locked boxes opening only to reveal another locked box inside, endlessly opening while bringing me no closer to an answer or to understanding.

All of this dispels as my eyes flick open to see Chaluay's face, so close to mine in the near-darkness. I move away and rub crusts from my eyes. "What time is it?" I ask. "What's the matter?"

"Wake up!" Chaluay's voice quivers with excitement. "We will be late!"

I tilt my watch toward the little bar of light cast on the floor by the outside streetlight. Now I understand why there is a big rock in the middle of my chest and silk stitching on my eyelids. "It's not even four in the morning! What are you talking about?"

"The river," she crows. "Remember? I told you I'd take you. Haven't you heard of the floating markets? That is where we will go. To see the river and to have a fine morning meal! It's quite a way out of the city, but it is an experience you should not miss."

I groan and try to roll over, but Chaluay has our day planned and will not let me spoil it. She chatters and chatters until I finally sit upright, wobbling slightly. There will be no more sleep for me this morning. I throw off my covers and shuffle toward the washroom and into the day.

We arrive at the river just before five o'clock. It's not raining yet, but the sky is inky black and the water looks like a giant mud puddle, hungry and slurping and smelling strongly of sewage. I shiver, wishing I were still curled up on my warm mat, wishing I were anywhere but here.

Chaluay parks her bike, and as we get nearer I can see that the river is full of winking lights. The water is afloat with so many tiny boats, and now the stench of sewage is overpowered by a whirlwind of delicious smells. In each boat I can see crates and crates of food. One boat holds ripe fruits; another, deep green vegetables; still another holds a small cookstove and an old woman stirring noodles in a precariously tilting pot. It is a floating food market, just as Chaluay said. The water all around is still big and wild and unfriendly, but I shut my eyes and breathe in the spicy smells.

Suddenly I am ravenously hungry. Chaluay tosses a few *baht* into the hand of a man standing at the ready with a small boat and she jumps in, calling out to me to join her. I shake my head and draw back. The food tempts me, but I will not go near that watery black mass. The very thought of it turns my bones to liquid.

Chaluay shrugs and I watch as she is maneuvered through the watery aisles, past other boats filled with silk and carved trinkets and silver jewelry. In a few minutes she returns with two plates of fish and rice. I thank her for her generosity and fall onto the best meal I have had since arriving in Bangkok.

As I eat, I turn my body so that the river runs behind me. It's bad enough to know it is there without keeping it in my sight every moment. Chaluay pauses, plastic fork halfway to her mouth, and looks at me.

"Did you buy many fancy things while shopping yesterday?"

I stare at her. Fancy things? What kind of person does she think I am? But of course, I realize, she doesn't know the real me. I've made sure of that. I frown at this fake persona I'm creating, and feel a second's desperate wish to tell her the whole truth. But what a crazy thought! She would just pity me, label me, maybe even shun me. With effort, I shrug and try for a secretive smile. And this fake smile makes me remember the day's real joy. I can't tell her about finding the key, but the other subject is safe. "I found a travel store."

"Oh?"

"Yes, a wonderful place—filled with posters from so many countries of the world!" I suddenly realize how eager I sound. How naive. I take a deep breath and slow my speech. "Not that it's anything special, of course, traveling around the world. On airplanes and—things like that." It's harder than I thought to show real enthusiasm while trying to be someone you are not. Obviously I need more practice at this. "Anyway, the man told me about a plane that goes to just the right place. It will take me home. And he said the money I have will be more than sufficient for the ticket."

I look at her expectantly, but she must not realize what a big deal this is. She is looking at me with a little frown, wrinkles creasing in between her eyes. After a minute I start to feel uncomfortable, but then she shrugs and brushes a few specks of rice off her lap. "That is good news. Well, when you are finished we should go back up the river a ways. There is something I want to show you."

I almost sigh with relief. Something happened a moment ago, and I am not sure what it was. Did she suspect me of keeping secrets from her? I'm glad to move on to safer subjects.

Even if the subject we are moving toward is the least safe thing I know.

Chaluay starts up her motorbike and we ride back into the city, then park near a bank of the Chao Phraya. The water roars louder here, and there is no way to walk right along the river's edge. Where could Chaluay be taking me? We approach the water, and I shift my position so that she walks nearest the bank. I want as much distance as possible from the rushing waves.

And then up ahead I see a fancy stone dock, with a fine-looking boat resting nearby. It is a busy area, with many people coming and going. The boat's motor roars loudly in the early-morning air. Up over the river, the sky is beginning to lighten. It will soon be dawn, but for now the shadows still hang thick around us. I try to keep my mind away from the menacing water and on the possibilities ahead. Keys and locks. Mysteries explained. Soon. Just as soon as the sun rises and the workday begins.

"See there?" says Chaluay, dragging me back to reality.

And the river. Shuddering a little, I follow the direction of her pointing finger. A man stands on the dock, bending in close to every person who approaches him. He takes some small thing they each put in his hand, then allows them to move past him, climbing over a narrow platform onto the boat.

Chaluay inches closer and I follow, warily. "Get ready," she says.

"Ready for what?" I ask. There is an awful clenching in my stomach, as I start to get a sense of what she has planned. Something I am sure I will hate.

She replies with a smile and a toss of her head. "A new experience, I'm sure. It will be good for you. Just be ready—and when I say the word, follow me. You need to be *fast*."

"Wait," I say, and grab Chaluay's arm. "I don't—"

But right then, a large group of people approach the man on the dock. They cluster around so that I cannot see him at all anymore. And Chaluay begins to move. "*Now!*" she hisses. She darts forward, and I follow her until we are very near the boat.

"What?" I say, panting.

"The ticket man will be distracted for another minute. We can slip on the ferry and no one will ever know. But you have to *move!*"

"I don't— I won't—" Terror steals my words and paralyzes my legs.

But Chaluay grabs my arm and yanks me firmly onto

the platform. "You have to come across," she says. "If they catch us now, they will arrest us. Do you want to go to prison?"

Chaluay has said the magic word. My legs turn into a blur of motion, and before I know it we have slipped across the platform and onto the unexpectedly wobbly deck of the boat.

"Quick," she says, and we duck down a dark flight of stairs just as the beaming sun peeps over the far horizon and floods the deck in a scarlet spotlight.

29

We stay hidden for less time than we spent preparing to sneak onboard the boat. Every corner is crowded with passengers, and no one gives us a second look. I am also interested to see that most of the people on the boat are *farang*. Many of these foreigners hold travel maps and lean far over the side of the boat, talking loudly and pointing and clicking their cameras in the direction of the rising sun.

As I stand and take in my surroundings, the rumbling of this great water beast grows louder. There is a lurch, and a man's voice comes out of a little speaker box in the corner of the room. He is telling us to find seats or stand up on deck to see the sights, telling us to enjoy this sunrise tour of Bangkok, City of Angels, telling us that the ride will last one hour and forty minutes . . . and here my heart begins to pound so hard I am afraid it will break free from my chest.

The boat's jolts have turned into strong, churning movements that tug us along on the rough water. Chaluay and I are well below the deck, but in my mind I can still see those hungry waves. They are the opposite of everything

I have known—they are free, unbound, stretching out so far in every direction—and the thought of all that wide-open space after the sturdy sameness of my upbringing is more than I can handle.

Chaluay does not seem to have noticed my distress. She is halfway up the stairs. "I do this all the time. They are so busy they never notice one or two extra people." She stops now, near the top step, and turns to look at me. For the first time, she falters. "Are you all right? Don't you like boats?"

Now there is a statement that should not be a question. I shake my head and push farther back into the wall. Slowly I sink to the floor, wrapping my arms around my knees, holding them tight against my wavering stomach. Maybe if I close myself up tight like this, I will be able to survive until we get back to dry land.

My eyes are squeezed shut and the boat jostles from side to side, so I don't notice right away that Chaluay has come back to sit on the floor next to me. I open my eyes and her face is soft and questioning.

"How are you going to get to America if you cannot travel by boat?" she asks.

That surprises me out of my discomfort and I look up at her. "By airplane," I say. "I told you."

She waves that aside. "Airplanes are very expensive. You say you have enough, but what if you run out of money? The boat is much cheaper. Safer, too. It takes only a little longer to get there."

I try to laugh at the thought of the word "safe" being

connected with this rickety vessel, but it comes out as a snort. Chaluay leans closer and gives me a tight smile. "You will be all right," she says. "I will sit here with you for a few minutes; then we will go up on deck. Together."

I groan, pressing my face into my hands. The world is still so new, so full of things that terrify me. Must I take handfuls of it all at once?

Chaluay's persistence and iron will help me, eventually, to move up the stairs and to the deck. My knees shake and my breakfast rises in my throat, but I breathe slowly and force myself not to give in to panic. And after a while I find that being able to see all that roaring water actually makes things easier. It brings my terror out of the shadows, lets me look on its face. And to my surprise, it is not as deadly as I had thought.

Once again I find that to see, to choose with open eyes, is far better than cowering in darkness, drowning in my fear.

I still cannot follow Chaluay to the guardrails, won't even watch as she reaches her arms out over the edge to try to touch the rising sprays of water, won't throw dry bread crusts to the catfish that cluster in gulping masses just outside the boat's wake. But I can bear to sit, far back from the edge, on a soft covered bench. And as the minutes tick away, I find I can smile at the early-morning sun's glow on my hands, at the fresh-scrubbed air, at the bustle of chattering languages and the raucous joy of a group of people doing something wonderful on a mild day.

Then the rain starts up and most of the people go inside, but when Chaluay stays on deck I don't even mind. I just sit and soak in the wet morning, and think how different some things are from how they seemed from a distance.

And when my feet finally cross the barrier to safety, I think that in another life, I might have grown to miss that boat's gentle rocking, so like the movement of my cot when I was very young, so like my mother's arms.

30

After our early-morning jaunt, Chaluay reminds me that she doesn't have all day to spend sightseeing. "Some of us have to work for our money," she says, and her tone has enough bite that I look up in surprise. But she just tosses me the spare helmet and kicks her bike engine to life.

She drops me on Rama IV with a good-bye as clipped and a look nearly as stony as on our first meeting with Kiet. "*Chok dee na ja*," she says, wishing me luck, but doesn't look like she really means it. What caused her to move from this morning's near-friendship back to this? I shake my head and push away the uncomfortable prickle at the base of my neck. I have bigger things to worry about.

Mostly: Rama IV is a longer street than I had expected, and I have been dropped off nowhere near BK Storage.

I set off walking.

My feet are sore by the time I see the tall Boss Towers building that was scribbled onto my map by the friendly travel man. From there it's just minutes to get to BK

Storage, a huge white box of a building with orange and blue trim on the edges. I stand outside for a long time, telling myself that just because it is shaped like a prison does not mean it will be the same on the inside. Finally I push open the front door and slip in.

And there I gasp. It's like moving from summer to winter in an eye's blink. A moment ago my arms were shiny with sweat. Now I can see every hair standing on end, and my back teeth start to clatter against each other. What is this strange frozen world? Even the coldest nights in my cell were nothing like this.

Unable to make sense of it, I move down the carpeted hall and come to a wide-open area where a young woman sits behind a gleaming wood desk.

"May I help you?" she asks in English.

I don't have any idea what to do, so I just pull out the key and place it on the desk in front of her. She picks it up and frowns, turns it over in her hands a few times. I try to imagine the key as seen through her eyes: the tendrils of rust curling along the teeth, the shriveled-up label, the cracked and peeling plastic. I sink a little lower where I stand.

"Will you wait a moment, please?" She gets up and slides out of the room.

I can't even imagine what's coming next. If this is my last clue and it goes nowhere, what happens then? But a minute later the young woman beckons me down another hallway. I enter a small bright office where a foreign man with pale hair stands frowning at me, holding my key.

"Good morning, Miss—?"

"Luchi Ann," I say, but I know this isn't enough. *Never reveal your full name*, Mama always told me. But how can I avoid it now? I settle on the next-best thing, though there is really no difference. "The key belonged to my mother. Her name was Helena Finn."

The man must notice my use of the past tense. "I'm so sorry," he murmurs. "Won't you sit down, Miss Finn? My name is Henry Rogers, and I'll help you sort this out. It's a bit of a problem, though—we haven't used this series of keys for nearly a decade. Do you know when your mother had a box with us?"

I drift into the chair he pointed out. Is this it, then? Nothing but a dead end? Have I spilled a lifetime's secret to a stranger for nothing? "Fourteen years ago," I say dully. I look at the carpet, tracing the curlicue pattern with my eyes, trying to keep back the blurry tears that threaten to spill out.

But Henry Rogers doesn't keep talking. He's looking at the key with a thoughtful expression. "Finn," he says. "Now, why does that name ring a bell?" He turns to the computer, types for a few minutes, then stands up and walks over to a big filing cabinet. As he pulls open drawers and shifts around the papers inside, he tosses an occasional look over his shoulder at me, keeping up a patter of conversation. "I've been doing this a long time, you know. Going on twenty years. And I see all types in this business— all types. We don't get many longtime customers, and I know I haven't ever had a Finn in here. But there's something that tickles at me, something— Ah!"

I look up, hardly daring to hope.

Henry whips out a yellowish folder. His eyes are bright. "Of course! Box 391—how could I forget? One of our regulars, he was. Nice young chap, drifted in and out occasionally, family business interests he was checking on here or some such. He liked to store things with us for safe-keeping, since he was in the country fairly often. Long-term fellow, always paid up regular from a dedicated account."

My mouth feels like it is full of dry lentils. I couldn't say a word if I tried.

"Last time he came through—right you are!—fourteen years ago, he added a name to the account: a certain Helena Finn." Henry looks up with a triumphant smile, takes in my expression, and returns hastily to his paperwork. "Special delivery, this one. Obviously important to him. Left it here and said he'd be back—but that's the last I ever heard. I always did wonder what became of him. He was paid up for the rest of the year, and truth be told, he had left enough in the dedicated account that the payments kept up automatically. We actually had those goods in storage as recently as six or seven years ago."

I open my mouth, but nothing comes out.

Henry's eyes are bleak. "I'm sorry, Miss Finn—Luchi. You have to understand, it's been so long. Unclaimed materials are recycled. The contents of that box just aren't around anymore."

But I hardly hear his last words. My thoughts are stuck back a few minutes ago, back at the first mention of that elusive *he*. There *is* a clue here, something immensely valuable to me, something I desperately need to know. I clear my throat, press my nails hard into the chair's leathery surface.

"Who—" My voice is hoarse and raspy. "He—you mentioned you knew the man who—who set up, who opened the account. Can you tell me—who he is? His name?"

Henry looks up in surprise. "Why, of course. Helena Finn was his wife, recently married I understood. So I assume that would be your father, wouldn't it? His name was Payne. Rupert Payne."

31

The rest of the day drifts by in a haze. I somehow make my way to Lumphini Park, where I connect with a bench and stare out across the lush green grass, seeing nothing. Rupert Payne, my father. Why did he never return for the items in his storage box? How did my mother end up with his key? Obviously there is some connection to Payne Industries, the company Jeanne talked about that so upset my mother. Could my father have been the one Mama feared so desperately? Is he the horrible, evil person she has been hiding from? If so, then why can't I suppress this desperate need to find him, to know him, to hear what he has to say?

I asked the man at the storage facility as many questions as I could think of, but his memory did not stretch to the kinds of details I need. Now I can think of a hundred questions I didn't ask, but I cannot return and face him again. I know I shouldn't be sitting here, wasting the day away. I know I should go back to the travel store, but I am so deeply sunk in my despair that I cannot bring myself to move.

And so I stay tangled in my thoughts, and by the time I see Chaluay's lean form beckoning me, I am no closer to unraveling them. For her sake I shake myself out of my stupor and try to paste on a cheerful expression.

But Chaluay seems to be in a funk of her own. As I climb on and settle my hands around her waist, she calls out, "Have you made plans for when you will leave Bangkok?"

I blush at her forwardness, but she hurries quickly along. "Only because I—I might need to travel soon. I will likely have to go out of town. So I just wondered if you— did you buy your ticket?"

"Not yet," I say, and then I feel suddenly angry with myself. Why, instead of spending the day dreaming of lost things, did I not go straight to Siam Square? First thing tomorrow, that's exactly what I'll do. "But very soon. I must go soon. Tomorrow I will buy the ticket."

And finally the knot in my mind untangles, and with that comes the peace I have been searching for all day. It's time to take the next step of my journey. I used the key. I didn't find any tangible treasure, no memento of my mother's past, but I did learn something important: my father's name. In spite of everything, my plan has grown stronger. I do have family, though they don't know it—and no one, not even Chaluay and her sour mood, can take my plan away from me.

Or so I think as I go to sleep that night.

. . .

The next morning, I am shaken awake again in the early dark, so that for a moment I wonder if perhaps I have been trapped in a never-ending yesterday. But Chaluay's look is not what it was; there is no sunrise on the river hiding in her gaze. Her look, from last night's pebbly stone, has gone to rock-hard flint.

"You must wake up," she says, shaking me again.

"I'm awake," I say, sitting up and pulling the cover around my shoulders, shivering in the chilly dark. Outside, thunder rumbles, and the rain roars like a waterfall.

Chaluay does not meet my eyes. Now that I am up, she backs away and scuffs toward the kitchen. "I am sorry," she says. "We must leave here now. I have had . . . unexpected news. I must leave town at once."

I gape at her. My mind is still fuzzy with sleep, and I am not sure what I am hearing. "But—"

"I am sorry," she says again. "But we must go very quickly. There is no time to do anything." She shoves my clothes at me, a neat folded pile. Did I leave them on the end of my bed, and not in my bag as I thought?

Still in the fuddle of sleep, I accept the clothes and go into the washroom to change. When I come out, she hands me a paper bag. "Food," she says. "This will last you today." She is looking everywhere except at me. I feel like I am back on the river, only now the boat is being peeled away, board by board, and the waves are roaring closer and closer. Outside the window, jagged lightning and cracks of thunder tear apart the sky.

Within minutes, we are out on the street. Chaluay's

bike roars through puddles, dashing the last bits of sleep from my foggy mind.

"Where do you need to go? Has something bad happened?" I call to Chaluay over the wind. But either she doesn't hear me or she chooses not to answer, and I do not repeat myself.

We are riding in a part of town that I have not yet seen. Everything around me gleams dark and wet. We are close to the river, but it is bigger and harsher than where we rode the ferry yesterday. I see many trucks and forklifts and, out on the water, ships so huge they look like floating barns. Has Chaluay brought me to the port? How will I get from here to the travel store?

The bike stops and I climb off, my mind whirling with questions. Chaluay does not follow me. Instead, she revs up the engine again. "I am sorry," she says quietly. For the first time since yesterday, she looks me full in the face, and my heart freezes inside me.

What is she not telling me?

Chaluay nods her head and roars away into the dark.

And as she goes, a flutter of memories come to me: Jeanne's warnings to always watch your back, no matter where you are. Chaluay's eyes, skittering guiltily around me, hurrying me out of her way. The travel man's angry hiss, telling me I should never carry around so much—

My hands, already wet but now ice-cold, fly to my bag. Ducking under an awning I claw open the top and pull out the tea box. My heart skips a beat to find it still there. Mama's papers. The letter. And the little pile of *baht* and—

The pouch that held my dollars, my ticket to freedom?

I pull everything out and rifle through it, check down to the bottom of the bag. But the pouch is no longer there.

Every last dollar is gone.

32

When I return to myself I am standing under the awning, frozen in place, clutching what is left of my life in my two arms. I still cannot believe it's true. Chaluay is not some street urchin, some common thief. She is a good friend of Kiet's, a girl not much older than me, someone who has shown herself to be playful and fun-loving. Someone I thought could become a friend. Was that all for show?

How could she rob me of my only means of getting home? Did she realize she was stealing away my last hope?

And my heart sinks further. She probably didn't realize. She had no idea who I was or how little I had. I made sure of that with everything I said and didn't say, made sure she thought I was some rich entitled foreigner.

But oh, that doesn't, couldn't ever excuse her! I throw my back against the wall, let the ground pull me down as I sink to my knees and pull up my hands to cover my head. It's gone. All of it. My plan, my hopes, my future.

Chaluay has stolen it all.

For a moment I think of trying to find her and explain—if she knew my situation, she would return the money, wouldn't she? But of course, this is impossible. What do I know of her house but a maze of Bangkok streets seen from the back of a speeding motorbike? I could go to her corner on Soi 2, but I know in my gut she won't be there to find. She and my dollars will be far away by this time.

I watch the wave of despair as it rolls closer. I drop my head and let it break over me, crushing me. For the first time since leaving Khon Mueang Women's Prison I feel completely and utterly lost. There is no one to fall back on. I think of Jeanne and Bibi and Isra. What would they say to me now? What would Kiet tell me if I called his mobile phone and told him what had happened?

What would Mama do? I reach a tentative hand into my bag and touch the bundle that holds the urn. In my mind I can see Mama's face—lined, strong, peaceful. I remember her last words to me. She said, *Go home*, but she said something else, too. *Be strong*, she told me. *Do what I could never do*. I remember Mama's tears and I see her terrified eyes, see the hope and strength that would build in her slowly, only to be dashed away every time she ventured to the computer and came face-to-face with her personal terror. That fear is here now, my own brand of it; I can feel it reaching for me, looking for a way into my soul.

But I cannot let it have me.

I must go on. No matter what becomes of me now, I

have to keep going. I know this with every breath that pulls through my body.

It may not be what Mama herself would have done. But it is what she told me. And it's what I must now do.

But how? Where? What hope do I have, with no money to take me anywhere? I lift my arms to wipe my face and pull my bag over my shoulder. Stepping back out into the rain, I look around me, taking in the trappings of the port, already busy in the early morning.

The port?

Was this Chaluay's try at an apology? Just how long was she planning this theft? I think back to her talk about boat travel, even showing me how to get onboard a ship without paying. Was that when she made up her mind to do this?

I dig inside me for anger, for rage, for the smallest trickle of hatred. But I am numb. Chaluay has left me with nothing.

Nothing but my loss, and a yawning emptiness.

For a long time I walk up and down the quay, looking with eyes that feel as empty as my insides. The sun has come up by this time, and the port is abuzz with activity. There are big trucks and little trucks, flatbeds loaded with boxes and machines with long cranes that swing metal containers high into the air.

And the ships! In the light they are like small countries, like all of Khon Mueang Women's Prison could fall inside and be lost forever. I wonder how those ships can stay afloat on the slippery surface of the water.

My hand strays into my bag. I feel for the tea box and pull it out—so much lighter, so empty without Mama's pouch. Closing my eyes, I reach inside myself and try to feel something, anything, to show me that I am still alive, that I really should keep going. But my heart is silent as a stone.

I open the tea box and look inside. The *baht* Isra left me are still there, but it is only a few hundred. From my time at the stores yesterday, I know this could buy me several nice sarongs, or a week's supply of cup noodles. It can be nowhere near enough to let me travel on one of these ships to America.

I look around for a smaller ship, one with tourists climbing on and off, though I hate to even consider following Chaluay's example. I hate that I seem to have no other choice. But the only people I see are wearing grubby overalls. They yell and sweat and lift and push. These are workers. The ships are not for carrying people at all.

I swallow tears and keep walking. As I pass each ship, I lean my head back to study it from top to bottom. Every one looks much the same, but I distract myself by reading the fancy painted names on the sides. The letters are printed big and bold and I like the way they put everything right out in the open for the world to see.

I pay special attention to the ships with English names. *Caledonia*, says the first. *Juniper*, goes another. *Southwestern Foghorn*, and *Tarantula Queen*, and *California Dreamer*.

I have walked on for eight or ten steps before I suddenly stop and turn back.

California? This is a name I have heard before. It's a place. I've heard Mama talk about this place, read about it in my textbooks. Even Bibi told me how she traveled there on vacation once, many years ago.

With a rush it comes back to me, and with it, a thin tremor of excitement. Of possibility.

California *is* a place.

A place in America.

I know that California is not the same state as Massachusetts, which is where my Mama was from. But it's a start. It's in America, after all. It cannot be far. Maybe I can walk from one place to the other once I arrive.

I have traveled from Khon Mueang Women's Prison all the way to Bangkok. I have come this far.

I could give up now, when everything seems so hopeless.

Or I could keep moving forward. I could try again.

I think for a long time about how I might get on the ship. It's clear that I cannot simply sneak onto this ship as Chaluay did the tourist vessel. This is not a boat jumble-packed with people, where a *farang* girl with yellow hair would not stand out or be noticed. This is a ship for carrying big objects.

As I watch, I see that what's being transported are huge metal boxes the size of our cell back on the inside. A giant crane lifts them, one by one, and drops them with a deafening clatter onto the deck of the wide, flat ship.

The ghost of an idea ripples through me. What if I could sneak into one of those boxes? I could slip inside, shut the doors, and be dropped right onto the ship's deck. It is not a bad plan. It is a plan that could succeed. But not right now. There are too many people around, too much activity.

So I sit in my corner, out of sight, watching the movement along the dock. I wait while the sun scoots across the sky and the crane starts and stops and the men run around and shout and call each other names in Thai that make my cheeks flush. I nibble the food Chaluay has left me, but I do not eat much. I don't know how long I will need it to last.

In the paper bag she has also put a plastic bottle of iced tea. I take one small sip and rub the last tear tracks from around my eyes. With this sweetness on my lips and the big ship before me, almost, almost I can turn my mind from Chaluay's betrayal and set my sights on the future.

33

I find my chance when the midday sun is high, wavering in the sky behind grim rain clouds. The dock is cleared out like the rice fields after harvest. On the far side of the cranes, a cluster of men eats from paper bags, but everyone else must have gone looking for market stalls.

I may not get another chance. I stand up and settle my pouch over my shoulder. I slip from my shelter into the light rain.

Up close, the containers are solid and tower high, giant boxes of rusty blue or red or green metal. They are shut tight with wide, heavy bolts. I reach the first one, but no matter how hard I tug at the front, it does not open. I try another, two, three more. Finally I throw myself at the doors, but still they do not budge.

My heart is sinking fast. Time is speeding and I can almost see the watery sun moving across the sky. In the distance, an engine roars back to life. Anytime now, the men will return to work. But I cannot give up. Not when I am so close. I move faster, shoving the door of each container in turn, yanking and pulling to see if maybe this one will let me in.

And then I see it: not a container at all, but a flat wooden pallet with low walls and no roof. It is piled with stacks of wooden crates and the crates are stuffed with cabbages. A heavy blue tarp is thrown over the whole pallet and tied down with cords as thick as my arm.

But not every corner is tied down. One edge is loose, flapping in the light breeze. I look both ways. Loud, brusque voices call out from somewhere nearby, but no workers are in sight. Not yet.

I take a deep breath. Then I grasp the plastic tarp with both hands, tug it up, and crawl underneath. Making myself small, so very small, I scramble over wood and cabbage and crawl-squeeze-push my way onto the pallet.

I pull the tarp down behind me, covering myself from sight.

The boxes on the pallet are piled every which way, in stacks both low and high. It's not hard to find a spot where two boxes are stacked next to six, and the blue tarp rises up into a tentlike spot just right for me to sit under. I make myself as comfortable as I can on the cold, lumpy bed. I reach behind to push against the tall stack. It feels sturdy, and the crates have a ridge all around the side so they can be stacked safely. At least I know they will not tumble over onto me when the pallet begins to move.

Then the deafening roar of the crane's motor starts up

somewhere nearby, and blind panic surges through me. I feel like my head will explode.

Before I have time to blink or react—change my mind, maybe, push through the opening and dart out, saying it was all a mistake—there is a terrifying jolt. Something slams into my hideaway.

My hands fly out to the side. I grab the edges of a plywood box so hard I can feel tiny splinters cut into my fingers. There is another, bigger jolt as something slides underneath the pallet. Then a sickening lurch, a clang . . .

And I am airborne.

For long minutes I feel myself swing from side to side. All morning I have watched this action unfold, the giant crane clamping onto containers and pallets, hoisting them high in the air, swinging them up and over the thin watery gap, then dropping them with a thud onto the waiting ship's deck.

I press my back into the boxes and hope that the stack will remain steady. I don't want to die crushed by cabbages. And here, swaying high over a space of nothing, a fit of hysterical laughter seizes me. I have come this far—I have done so much—and here I am, dangling in the air like a worm on a hook.

Slowly, forcefully, I loosen my grip on the sides of the box. I pull my knees into my chest. I make myself breathe in and out. The churning in the pit of my stomach slows, though I can still feel the air swirling outside my floating nest.

There is a click and a whir and a pause—and I reach down and grab the sides again just in time. My stomach does a complete somersault as my pallet is released from the crane and plummets down to the waiting deck. I hit with a jolt that throws my head back against the plywood and leaves me gasping for breath, my neck aching and my jaw tightly clenched.

I can no longer hear the crane's motor. The men's voices are a distant memory. But now there is a new sound, and it is heat and stink and motion all together. It is a low, grating rumble that comes from somewhere deep below me.

It is the ship's motor, gearing up for departure.

There is truly no turning back.

34

Long after that last freefall, I stay folded in on myself. There is a tender spot on the back of my scalp and splinters in my palms and a throb in my neck. But for now, I am safe. The cabbages underneath me are smooth stones; the tarp overhead is a tent to keep out trouble. Time blurs. My early wake-up this morning blends with all the tension and action and high emotion of the past hours, lulling me into a trance, pushing my worries into the background.

I sleep.

When I am jolted awake, at first I don't know what has woken me. My fingertips are tingling and my ears are ringing. My wide eyes gobble up my strange surroundings. This cocoon of blue, this warm nest, with the soothing pitter-patter just inches from my face—what is all this? For long seconds, my mind is an empty wall.

It is all starting to come back to me when a sound rips through my mind. It's some kind of horn, I can tell right away, but like nothing I have heard before. This must be what awoke me from my sleep. The sound is low and guttural, and seems to come from deep in the belly of this great ship-beast I am riding, merging sound and smoke and grinding gears into one earth-shaking noise that sets my whole body trembling.

Then we are moving.

And suddenly I am glad for this noise, this horrible bellowing that feels like a knife through my mind. I am glad, because as long as I am busy fighting off the assault of that sound, I can't think about that narrow stretch of water that separates the ship from the shore. That trickle of water that will become a pool, that will become a lake, that will become an ocean bigger than my whole world, that could swallow me into nothing, that could drown me without a second thought.

My ship is leaving the harbor. My real journey has begun.

And this is how the time goes.

I don't know what part of the ship my pallet has been placed on, but the voices, when they come at all, are faint and indistinct. I nibble bites of the food Chaluay left me, ration myself to tiny sips of the tea. When the morning light shines bright through the tarp, I can see inside my little room. During this time I study the letter from my grandmother, puzzling over its meaning.

I think about Mama and her secrets. I think, once again, of my father. All my life Mama lived in a prison filled with women, but I know that my beginning cannot have taken place there. I have counted back the months, and I know that she already carried me inside her when she was arrested.

And this brings me back to Rupert Payne. I whisper his name over and over to myself, like I am searching it for some hidden meaning, some clue to his nature or whereabouts.

Growing up without my father was not difficult. I had a mother, many mothers, and all the care and nurturing I wanted. What more could I need? But now I am alone. Now my bars are gone and so are all my mothers. In this cold new world, I could learn to like having a pair of strong arms behind me, holding me up, protecting me.

But again, the letter haunts me. "That monster of a man," my grandmother said. What if she was referring to my father? What if he was the unspeakable terror who broke my mother's mind and flung her to this strange refuge at the end of the world? Or . . . what if my father is still out there somewhere, wishing and wondering about me, as I am about him?

This last thought trembles through my mind, timidly at first, then gaining force. And like a shiver that grows strong with the cold, my need surges and swirls and threatens to swallow me. It is the wanting that gives it strength, I know, and I can see that it's as much of a fantasy as my Cinderella dreams of someday finding a home, a happy ending, getting answers to my lifetime of secrets. With effort, I force the thoughts away and anchor myself in the now.

Outside, the night has fallen with the wind's whisper kiss. The deck is perfectly silent, has been for hours. My paper bag holds only a few leftover crumbs. The tea is long gone. My stomach cramps with hunger. How long have I been in this tent, sitting alone, dancing with my thoughts? I know I have passed at least three nights, but with the way my world blurs, it might have been more. I sleep some and then awaken, talk to myself and try not to listen too carefully to the answers.

I think of Kiet and the way his look held mine, like I was a very small sculpture, finely carved and easily breakable. I wonder if he was right to think this, or if there's more to me than that, if there is something inside me that won't break, that will go on no matter what, that will push through storm and fire to reach my goal. There are times I have felt this want like a hard stone pushing me on. But other times I just feel tired, and alone, and afraid.

Near me lies one cabbage, plucked halfway to its core. I pull another crunchy leaf close to my lips, shear it with small, neat bites. It gives me both food and drink, but I fear it may not be enough. Already my jaws ache with crunching, and my throat feels parched and raw.

When the night is darker, I will crawl out of my hole, as I have done several times so far. On these forays I find a dark corner to empty my aching bladder. I stretch my legs and teach them how to walk again after the long cramped hours in one position. I put trembling hands on the rail and turn my face into the foam-spattered darkness that holds my terror and my deliverance, my way to safety.

I hold my face into the wind and I stand there until the shivering stops and I can persuade myself, for one stinging moment, that I am not afraid.

PART III

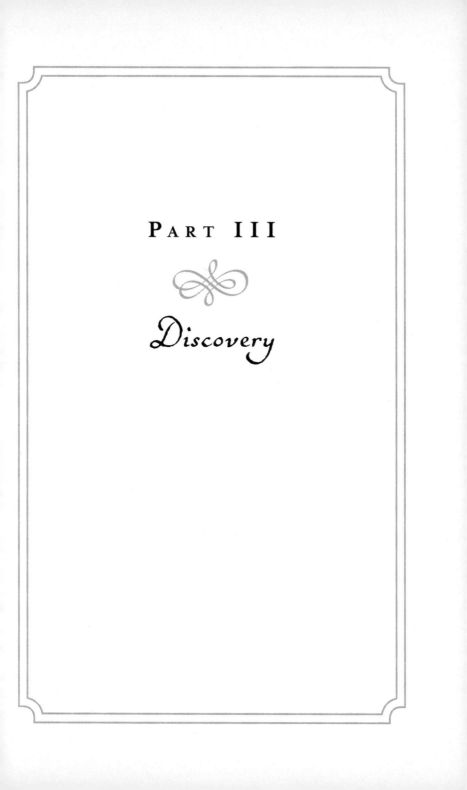

Discovery

35

Deliverance, when it comes, is sharp and sudden. It starts with footsteps growing steadily nearer, and I know then what is coming. There's a swish and a groan and a sudden burst of light, and then a bold, strong gasp of air lands on me like a slap.

I squint into the sudden pool of brightness. A man's voice yells, then falters, and then the cover drops over me again. Cringing into myself, I squirm farther back on my pallet, try to push myself out of sight.

I've been discovered. What will become of me now?

I feel like a cornered animal, and my panic is so strong it blinds my eyes, steals my tongue, paralyzes every muscle in my body. Blood pounds in my ears and in the time-frozen silence I can hear the *thump, thump, swish* of my heartbeat rising and falling.

A white cloud of fear swirls toward me and I want nothing more than to fall into it, lose myself in its blank emptiness. But the cloud becomes a screen and on the screen I see images. Me. My life. Through the pounding of my heart I remember everything that's happened since I left the prison. I remember Mama.

And I see her as she so often was: her wide, terror-struck eyes as she grappled with some nightmare, as she lay still inside her life and let fear hold her captive. I see her beaten not by prison but by her own refusal to fight. And I finally see the truth: Mama gave up on her life.

But what about me? I think of myself, the paths I've traveled and the distance I've come. I remember the danger on the road to Sukhothai. I remember arriving at the port, alone, betrayed. I was afraid, but I didn't lie down and quit. I didn't give up then and . . . the knowledge hits me like a bucket of icy water, waking me out of my stupor.

I won't give up now, either. I won't. I can't let my fear hold me down. Not now; not ever again.

Whatever is to come, I must face it.

I don't have long to wait. The bellow of voices gets louder; then my covering is pulled all the way off. Black-stained hands drag me to my feet and tug me onto the deck. More lights point at me now, three or four bright beams coming from different directions. Then two of the lights turn away and a rough brown arm reaches out and grabs hold of my shoulder, tries to yank me forward.

My legs crumple under me. Is it from fear? Hunger? Weakness after being hidden so long? I've got to stand up. I've got to be strong.

Four sailors loom on all sides of me. I push my palms onto the deck, stand up on wobbly legs. The nearest man digs callused fingers into my arm, half tugging, half carrying me along the deck and through a rusty metal door, where I nearly topple down a long flight of stairs.

The man behind me grabs my other arm, and together the two keep me upright. My shoulders ache and my head pounds, so I shut my eyes and just try to keep up. And then I'm in a room, propped up on a narrow seat that leans against the wall. Three of the men are gone, but the fourth glares at me. His hands open and close like he is looking for something to throttle. He glares at me through blood-shot eyes.

"Stowaway," he says to me in broken English. "Much bad, very bad. You see captain now. Very bad, much danger. Captain very much punishment."

I turn my eyes from the sailor's burning look, and after another minute he stomps away.

I am alone. Again.

The room I am in is sparse, with two chairs clamped to the floor and a bare countertop. A small round window shows the blackness of the outside. I am looking out of it, trying to find stars in the night sky, trying not to think about where I am and what will happen next, trying to cling to my hope, when there is a noise behind me.

The door opens with a sharp click.

Footsteps.

The captain has arrived.

Where is that strength I've only just found? Where is my backbone when I need it? My eyes are glued to the window. I can't move a muscle.

"You there!" grates a harsh voice. "Who are you? Why are you here?"

It's useless to delay what must be done. I take a deep breath and turn to face the captain.

And then I freeze midturn.

I don't know what I was expecting, but this is not it. The man in the doorway is no taller than I am, and has the frame of a boy. He's got very pale skin and his shock of gray-white hair is topped with a captain's hat that looks comically large. Even his clothes look too big. But his mouth is turned down at the edges, a stringy gray mustache quivers, and his eyes look like exploding firecrackers.

The first shock of unreality is followed by a lurch in my stomach as I look into his eyes. I see no softness, no mercy there. Whatever his size, this man means business.

"Who are you and what are you doing on my ship?" The captain's voice booms so loud that I start to shake. Instinctively I bring my hands together and bow my head in a *wai*. He probably won't know the traditional Thai greeting, but it soothes me. And hides my face for one precious moment while I try to gather myself.

"Sir—" I begin, trembling a little, but he cuts me off. His voice rises to typhoon level.

"Do you have any idea how many stowaways try to sneak

on my ship at every port of call? Do you know how much each one costs me? The trouble and paperwork and money it takes to get them sorted out? Do you want to know what I did with the last stowaway? Huh?"

I flinch as horrible images flash through my head. What *does* happen to stowaways on a ship? Do they get thrown overboard? Put to work as slave labor? Locked up in a dark prison cell?

A shudder goes through me as I picture myself returning to prison, only this time as a real inmate, this time all alone. I ball my hands and force myself to keep taking slow breaths. What can I do?

The captain marches closer. Suddenly he stops, a puzzled look on his face. He leans forward and grabs my chin, turns it from side to side. "How old are you, girl? You look like a child. Are you here alone?"

I shiver.

So this is it. The moment of truth. Where is that new girl inside me, the one with no stain on her past, the one with all ordinary answers to so many difficult questions? Can that girl save me now? Could she ever?

Because suddenly it seems to me that what brought me here, to this place, has a lot to do with my trying to be someone I'm not. Chaluay. Who was I to her? Some *farang* loaded with money—or so it would seem from the stories I told—and easily able to get more. I think back to those conversations when I lived out my make-believe life, drawing in bits and pieces of it whenever the mood struck me.

If I had done things differently, would Chaluay still have acted as she did?

There's no way of knowing. But one thing I do know. I'm tired of pretending.

The room has gone quiet. I look at the captain and something I now see in those fireball eyes—some spark of warmth or understanding—gives me courage. Surely this strange boy-man with the larger-than-life voice has had his own share of difficulties in life. Maybe he, of all people, could understand mine. All the times I've closed my lips and held in my secrets, what was really the point? What good did it do me?

I'm sorry, Mama. I've tried—I really have. But this world is not like the inside. I can't fight my battles with fantasy. I am not you. I have to work things out in my own way.

With a deep breath, I decide to take a chance. I decide to risk everything I have on a handful of whispered words. I break the final taboo and, for the first time in my life, speak aloud my full name.

"My name is Luchi Ann Finn," I begin. "I am thirteen years old and I was born in the Khon Mueang Women's Prison."

The ship pitches and tosses, so much so that I hardly notice the sticky web of secrets break loose around me as I push through and lay my life bare before this stranger.

But it feels magical.

I am like a bottle kept so long closed in on itself, but once open, unable to be corked again. Words spill out of me like water, pouring over my lap, over the floor, over and around and through my listener. And the captain looks at me, wide-eyed, mouth open. After a few minutes he drops down in the chair opposite me, pulls a silver flask out of his jacket, and takes a drink.

"Go on," he booms, and I do.

I tell him about Mama, about her secrets, about my grandmother's letter. I talk about Kiet and Chaluay and how I came to be sleeping with the cabbages on his boat. I talk until my throat feels like dried fish and every word comes out with a crackle. I talk until the sky outside the little round window glows pink and shiny, and the captain still sits next to me, shaking his head, turning his now-empty flask over and over in his lap.

It doesn't seem to occur to him to doubt my story. Maybe it's too fantastic to be anything but true, sitting here as we are, in a wood-paneled room on a container barge in the middle of the Pacific Ocean. One black dot in a sea of blue; two strangers tossed together by circumstance, and finding—just for a moment—a connection and kinship they had not even known they were looking for.

36

My story is finished, and at first the captain sits dazed. Then he leaps up and starts pacing back and forth, crackling with energy. Before my eyes he transforms from hunter to protector.

"My dear," he says. "Never in my life have I heard such a tale! Astounding! But don't you worry yourself—no, you've come to the right place. How you came to be here—bah!" He puffs a little, like an annoyed dragon. "That so-called friend . . . such treachery! Bald thieving!"

How quickly he has forgotten my own dishonesty, in his concern over the wrongs done to me. My eyes fill with tears.

"The *California Dreamer* is outfitted to hold fifteen passengers, fifteen paying guests we can carry as well as a full complement of goods. And how many are on board now, you ask? Hah!" The captain slaps his knee in a triumph of his own genius. "Six! Six passengers on board, and so we have plenty of room for you, my girl. No, say no more. You'll be my guest and I'll not hear of anything different. In fact, I have just the place to put you—a charming stateroom on the upper deck that will suit you perfectly.

"Well?" he barks, pausing midstep. "What do you think of that, eh? I'll have you outfitted in no time. Right as rain, you'll be. No need to worry about a thing. What do you say to that, girl, eh? Luchi—that's your name? Luchi, a fine name. Can't say I've heard it before, but it rings strong, yes sir it does."

"I am overwhelmed," I say. "I fear I will not be able to repay you. I do have some *baht*. It's not much, but . . ."

"Tosh and nonsense," he blusters, going red in the cheeks. "Of course you're not going to pay me. You will be a guest on my ship—a guest, do you hear? I won't have it be said I took money from an impoverished child, no sir, not Captain Jensen! It's the least I can do after all you've been through, and that's a fact. Now, up you get, girl. Let's move you along to the dining hall." He looks at me and lifts a burly eyebrow. "No. I think the stateroom first. You'll want to get cleaned up. Follow me."

With that, the captain yanks open the door and marches out into the hall, leaving me wondering: What just happened? Did my story somehow cut through his crusty exterior to find the hidden warmth? Could it be that all it took to put my life back on course was a long shot of the truth? After all the strange turns my road has taken, I don't know how to handle this sweeping kindness.

"Who are you?" I ask the empty room the question

I would not dare ask the captain to his face. "Are you some kind of a fairy godmother?"

Saying this out loud makes me giggle, and in the distance I hear the captain's voice booming: "Now, where's that young girl gone and put herself?"

I jump to my feet, slip my bag over my shoulder, and step out into the hallway. It's easy enough to follow him. His stream of words floats along like a guide rope through the corridors, leading me around unfamiliar cabins, through narrow halls, with the ship swaying gently around me.

For a second I think back to that moment I first set foot on a boat with Chaluay, and am surprised that I no longer feel the least bit afraid. It turns out that deep water—much like the truth about my past—wasn't there to drown me at all, but to bring me where I needed to go.

37

It is easier than I expect to fall into the ship's routine. It's a carefree life: all the structure and boundary of the inside, blown through with the salt tang of freedom, the knowledge that this small moving world is mine to explore, to navigate, to possess. That it is not only sheltering me, but also driving me toward my goal.

The stateroom the captain has promised me is enormous. This whole wide space—all for me? I count careful steps down the center of the room, from one side to the other. I measure ten paces one way and twelve the opposite. It is so much bigger than the room I grew up in, and that was always swarming with people. The bed is as big as three of my old prison cots, and it is up off the ground almost to my thighs. A colorful bedcover is draped over it, and when I peek underneath I see a smooth-sliding drawer: empty, inviting me to fill it with treasures.

The floor is covered with a deep brown fur, and after I have measured the room I kick off my sandals and spend long minutes treading back and forth, tangling my toes in its plush covering and trying not to laugh out loud. So this is the miracle of carpeting!

There is more to the room, much more, and it takes me several hours to explore it to my satisfaction. Once that is conquered I venture out to other parts of the ship: the kitchen with its sweaty, noisy bustle; the navigation deck, where the captain pulls up a stool for me and launches into long historical and scientific lectures; the lounge, where I make the timid acquaintance of Mr. and Mrs. Rosenberg, retired globe-paddlers and self-appointed freighter-travel experts, who are authoring their third highly acclaimed book on the subject.

And there is the rec room, so called not because it has been wrecked, as I first thought, but short for "recreation," which is a word I did not find much use for growing up. This room is full of brightly colored game boxes, paperback books, a television larger than the window of my old cell, and stacks of movies and video games. This room terrifies me. I feel its magnetic tug but I cannot follow it. With such a glut of information, how could I possibly know where to begin? How could I keep from being buried by the mountain of things I do not know, that I cannot ever hope to catch up on?

These questions do not seem to bother Captain Jensen. He takes my gaps in stride and makes it his business to compress a lifetime of missed opportunities and knowledge into three weeks of travel by sea. There seems to be no time when his lips are not moving. It occurs to me at some point that it was a good thing I got my whole story out that first day, for I have hardly been able to speak six words together to him since.

But my mind is wild with new knowledge. I learn about the sea and the different types of freighters, of which the break-bulk, or general cargo (into which category falls the *California Dreamer*), is the vastly superior, in that it can load free goods as well as containers. While more and more freighters are reformatting to transport only containers, Captain Jensen tells me he sees the value in maintaining some of the old sense of tradition, and that he has made a fine business so far in giving value to big and small vendors alike, not only those who have the money and means to hire at the top of the line.

I learn about satellites, those hidden machines that loop the earth so far out of sight which have put the old navigational tools almost completely out of business. The satellite is a further boon, the captain explains, because it allows for phone and limited Internet usage, despite being so far out at sea. This is no small miracle, he assures me, and looks over to see if I am suitably impressed.

I consider this. "My set of encyclopedias was published in 1986," I say. "My grasp of technology is . . . limited." I am being generous, of course. I have seen the computer in Chief Warden Kanya's office, the one my mother was given special privileges to use twice a year, but I was never allowed to touch it myself. One magazine sent to Jeanne by her cousin contained an article debating companies named Microsoft and Macintosh, and meant nothing to me. I know computers are information machines, but in Mama's case they only launched her into weeks of dark depression. What could I want with such a device?

Captain Jensen looks thoughtful. "Nineteen eighty-six?" he asks. "Well, we shall have to remedy that somehow. But tell me, have you been in the rec room yet?"

I lower my head, shake it just barely. I hope he will not probe further.

But this is Captain Jensen, after all.

"All right," he says. "Out with it, girlie. What's eating you?"

I sink lower in my chair, but seconds tick by and I am so shocked at his sudden silence that I have to put out words to fill it. "It's a lovely room," I try. "But it's just . . . too much. There is too much there. I don't know where to start."

That's all I can manage, and I am not sure if he will understand. But he nods.

"Ah, of course. Too bloody much information. And why not? A girl can't chow down a whole supermarket in one sitting, can she? And who would expect it? Well, my dear, I have an idea. We'll have things sorted out for you in no time. Nineteen eighty-six? My, my!" He shakes his head and his muttering trails off under his breath.

In a few minutes we are back to the history and development of satellite technology, but when I return to my room after dinner that night, I find that someone has been there before me. On my bed I see a small pile of books.

I approach, lift the first one reverently, as if it might explode in my hands, or maybe light a fire that will never go out again. I trace my finger along the titles, inspect each one: *A Tale of Two Cities. Charlotte's Web. Harry Potter and the Sorcerer's Stone.* I flick open this last one—it is a silly name that makes me want to laugh. And before long I am drawn into this story of a child who has grown up in one world, never dreaming that one day he would learn about another one so completely different from all he has known, so full of wonders, a world where every hidden dream has the chance to come true.

After that, a new book or magazine is on my bed every time I come into my room. Some have faded cloth covers and gilt writing. Others are soft paperbacks and have photographs of girls with red lips and shiny hair. Some are magazines from one, two, or six years ago. I read names of people I have never heard of, learn what they ate for breakfast and how often their shirts have come untucked from their skirts, and who was caught walking in public with toilet paper stuck to her shoe. It all seems so trivial. When I was growing up, many inmates were obsessed with analyzing and gossiping about what their cellmates or others said and did. It was a way of passing the time, putting a lens up to our tiny world and finding out what crawled under every rock. But I am shocked to find that same thing here, on the outside.

Maybe some things don't change no matter where you are.

I soon begin to set those magazines aside unopened. It's the books that really tug me under. Most of what I read is new to me, but some stories I have heard before, in Bibi's croonings, in Mama's bedtime tales, even some books I owned or borrowed and read on the inside. These existing pieces frame my growing knowledge, make the new portions fit better. Slowly, one bit at a time, I feel the world beginning to take shape around me. It is a fascinating course of discovery, and before long I find myself with a huge stack of completed items.

One day soon, I decide, I will go into the rec room. Only to return things. I won't stay; I will just walk to the door and slide in the books I have read. Or maybe I could walk inside, just as far as the bookshelves. Just to make sure that every book I have been given is filed back in its proper place.

Maybe, if something catches my eye, I might also leave with one or two new books to read. Books that I have picked out for myself.

"So how are you faring?" the captain asks me a few days later, as we sit at dinner with the ship's first mate, Ahmed, and the Rosenbergs. "Enough to do? Your room to your satisfaction? Explored every nook and cranny of the place yet?"

"Oh yes, it is all wonderful. Thank you," I murmur into my bowl of split-pea soup. And it's true. He's been so generous and welcoming I sometimes feel embarrassed by it.

"That's just capital. But I'd do anything for you, Mandy, you know that."

Mandy? I look up. Captain Jensen's face has gone ghost-white. The spoon he is holding drops from his hand and clatters down onto his plate. Thick green soup splatters all over the tablecloth.

"Captain?" I say.

But he jumps up, pushes away from the table, and dashes off across the dining room. I look around the table. "What just happened?"

The others exchange glances. Then Ahmed says, "Mandy was Captain Jensen's daughter. She died two years ago."

Mrs. Rosenberg reaches over and puts her hand on top of mine. "It's been so good to have you here, darling. This is our third trip with Captain Jensen, and the first time we've seen him the way he was *before*. He's been almost . . . happy. You've done this for him. I think he's just so glad to have a child around again."

Missing pieces fall into place in my mind, and suddenly the captain's immediate welcome, his unconditional acceptance, makes a lot more sense. But at what price has come my rescue? I stand up and push my chair away from the table. "Please excuse me," I say. "I'm not hungry anymore."

I know that whatever happened to Mandy Jensen wasn't

my fault, but I can't help feeling guilty. Her death, after all, has contributed to my own good fortune. And this makes me feel like the worst kind of thief. I walk past the captain's stateroom, but his door is open and the room is empty. Where would he be? I drift up one hall and down another, but he's in none of his usual places. Finally I come out on deck and there he is, on the bridge, looking out over the water.

He half turns his head, and smiles when he sees that it's me. "Luchi," he says. "I'm so sorry. Shameful display, what you saw down there. I can't excuse myself. It's just—" His voice breaks a little and I rush over, put my hand on his arm.

"I'm sorry, Captain Jensen," I say. "The others told me about—about . . ."

He wipes his eyes and laughs a little. "It's okay. You can say her name. Mandy was more full of life than anyone I've ever known. She . . . she would have been eleven this year. This month."

There's nothing I can say to that, so I just squeeze his arm a little harder. He reaches into his shirt pocket and pulls out a picture of a girl with light brown braids and laughing green eyes. She looks so alive that it takes my breath away. And I never even knew her. How does he go on?

I think of Mama. How alive she was . . . until she wasn't. I remember my own picture, the one in my tea box, the one I've held through so many days, soaked with tears so many nights. And just like that, my feelings of guilt are gone. I haven't stolen anything from Captain Jensen, any more than he has from me. I'm not his Mandy, but if he can find some laughter in my eyes, if I can find some shelter in his words, then maybe—even just for a short time—both of us can feel that we've never really left home. That life can still go on.

38

After that day, Mandy gradually becomes a part of our daily conversations. "You should read this—it was her favorite book," the captain would say. Or, "That's just the sort of thing Mandy would do!" Or, "Well, my girl, as I told Mandy the first time she fell and scraped her knee . . ." To my surprise, I find I enjoy these little reminiscences; I like learning about this girl who, if she were alive, might not be too different from me. I've never had a friend my age, but some nights, alone in my stateroom, I imagine her sitting next to me, reading or talking or playing a game. It's almost as good as the real thing.

Mandy isn't the only thing we talk about, of course. The subject of computers fascinates Captain Jensen endlessly, and he devotes much time to trying to help me understand these complicated machines. It's no use. Computer is another language, and it's clear to me that I will never be fluent.

And so the captain sets his considerable energy into changing this, too.

Ten days into our journey, there is a loud clatter outside my cabin. I set aside the book I'm reading and open the door. Captain Jensen bursts in like a whirlwind, holding a flat silver machine in his outstretched arms. He sweeps over to my small desk and gets very busy with cords and cables, whirling around like the genie in the book I have just put down.

Finally, after about fifteen minutes of effort during which he neither stops talking nor says a single thing about his purpose, he turns to me and beams in triumph.

"There," he says. "You're all set—right as rain."

I look blankly at him.

"It's an ancient Dell—nearly six years old, I'm afraid, and slow as molasses. Can't get any of the crew to use it anymore. Been on the scrap heap since Christmas. But she runs—and she's all hooked up to the 'net, too. Come here, I'll show you how she purrs."

The lid is up on the machine and the screen is alive with movement, words and colors and chirrups of sound. I am starting to understand what he is doing.

"Whatcha say?" he asks. "Your very first computer!"

What can I say? I am unable to form any words at all. But the good captain does not give me or my speechlessness any consideration. He sits me down in the chair and sets about enlightening me to the mysteries of the big spider's web called the Internet. All of his chattering about satellites, apparently, was leading toward this moment where, though we are in the middle of the ocean, the computer is able to link up with many others all around the world. The connection isn't fast, he assures me, but it is reliable. He's told me much of this information before, but now, looking at the screen and touching the keys with my own fingers, it begins to make slow sense.

By the time several hours have passed I am starting to understand how this machine works and what goes where and does what. Captain Jensen teaches me how to send letters by e-mail and how to find information with search engines, and a whole string of lightbulbs in my head goes off at once.

Suddenly, I cannot wait until he is gone. I begin to twitch with possibility, but the captain is still full of things to say. Another long hour passes before a knock at the door recalls him to his duties. He nods curtly at the intruding seaman, then beams at me. "Well, then, you're getting the hang of it, aren't you? I have to run along now—the navigation deck's probably come all apart with me being gone so long. You explore all you like. Who knows what you might find out there on the web?"

He winks and zips out, leaving me to my new typing machine, with dozens of little gray keys that talk to me, that tell me they are going to open doors for me, so many doors that I did not even know existed.

First I pull out the paper Kiet left me and begin to type him an e-mail. It is a brief note, and I feel awkward and embarrassed to be putting my thoughts out in such a public way. Could not anyone find the letter and read it? It takes me a long time to move the words from my mind to my fingers, but the more I do, the easier it gets. I decide not to tell Kiet about Chaluay's betrayal and why I ended up traveling by boat instead of by plane. Chaluay must find her own path, after all. I won't let her consume any more of mine. There is still plenty to say, and by the time I am happy with my note and hit *Send*, I feel a warm glow of satisfaction in my middle.

I realize that for the first time I have passed the start of lunch without noticing. I don't even feel hungry.

I close the e-mail window and see the search engine, left open from Captain Jensen's tutoring session. A name flashes through my mind, the name at the top of the letter I have read so often I could recite it from memory. I know what I need to do.

With quivering fingers and a hurricane in my chest, I tap out the letters and watch the blinking cursor form the words: *Mrs. Regina Finn.*

Please wait, the computer tells me, and I do. I know that it is not taking longer than normal, that it is only the slow connection the captain has described. But in my mind I imagine the invisible currents of wind striking bargains with the gods of information, deciding how much to parcel out, what to give and what to keep hidden away.

Another second passes and a torrent of information scrolls across my screen: 22,037 results. I force myself to breathe slowly. Then I get another idea. I return to the search window and type again. The more information, the better, right?

No more secrets.

Mrs. Regina Finn. 21 Stafford Circle. Brookline, Massachusetts.

I hold my breath.

Thirty-two results.

I click on the first one.

It opens up into a peach-and-lavender montage of photos and animation: *Welcome to the personal home page of Gina Finn.*

39

It is almost too much to take in. When I finally creep into the dining room for lunch, Captain Jensen narrows his eyes and waves his fork at me. "Luchi, my girl—what's come over you? Something momentous, I know. Something big. Something superlative! Out with it. What's eating you? Some news? Some discovery?"

I just shake my head and slide into my seat.

But, of course, it all comes out soon enough. And the more the minutes tick away, the more excited I am with my discovery. I tell him about finding my grandmother's web page, about the photos I have seen and everything I have learned about this severe, smiling woman with the iron-gray hair and the steely eyes. It is a new experience, finding this window into an unknown world. The perspective sits on me like a gown that doesn't fit right, this one-way knowing that takes but doesn't give, that doesn't reach all the way to the person being known. I wonder if, today, sitting on the far side of the ocean, my grandmother might look into her computer screen and see, just for a moment, the reflection of my eyes studying hers.

The captain is delighted with my discovery and makes me repeat her name and address so he can write it down in the spiral notebook he carries in his shirt pocket. Then he caps his pen, stows his notebook, and tugs on one corner of his mustache. Elbows on the table, tapping both hands together over his dish of blueberry pie, he looks right in my eyes and asks the question.

"Have you tried to look up information about your mother?"

The question is like a gust of icy wind—cold, unexpected, taking my breath away.

He looks down. I suppose he can see how his words have affected me. In true form, he fills the awkwardness with more talk. "I know she was . . . er, gone away from home most of her life. Her adult life. But you never know what a search can turn up. There might be information about her . . . about the events that led to her being . . ."

For maybe the first time since we've met, Captain Jensen's words fail him. But they are enough for me. Why didn't I think of this myself? It should have been the first thing to enter my mind. I see that now. But somehow, I still can't quite believe it's possible. That it could be so easy.

I push back my half-empty soup bowl and stand up. The ship lurches and I steady myself on the table, try not to look like I'm stumbling around in panic, in anticipation—or maybe in joy. But why should I feel any of those emotions?

Do I really think the answers to my life's secrets are so easy to find?

There's only one way to find out.

With a smile for the captain, I turn and bolt back out of the dining room, down the narrow ship's corridors, and into my room. I collapse at the keyboard and unload a flurry of strokes onto it. It takes a few tries to get the combination right, but I am improving.

The string of hits rolls down the page like a breaking ocean wave. Words jump out at me, stinging me with their sharp, pointed edges. DISGRACE! SCANDAL! TRAGEDY!

And another word, a name I have heard before, one that I somehow knew would be at the heart of this mystery: Rupert Payne.

Taking a deep breath, I click on the first link. It is a small portion in the gossip column for some online periodical. Mama's name leaps out at me: ". . . young unknown named Helena Finn . . ."

I force my eyes back to the beginning of the article.

Word on the street is: the Battle for the Bachelor is *on*. This year's Most Eligible Bachelor and heir to Daddy's billion-dollar tech industry fortune, Rupert Payne Jr. has been linked to society's best and brightest. There were even whispers of an engagement to society princess Jocelyn Lennox as recently as last month.

But now there is a new player on the scene, digging in with sharp and allegedly fortune-hungry talons.

The lady in question is a young unknown named Helena
Finn, 20, of Brookline. Are the two a couple? Only time
will tell. And oh . . . whatever will Daddy say to that?

My heart is pounding a marathon. The article moves
on to other, juicier subjects, but I squint at a thumbnail-
sized photograph on the screen. A tall, dark-haired man
with flashing eyes and slicked-back hair poses for the camera. On his arm is a slender young woman. She has her
head arced away from the camera, turned in toward the
man's chest.

But her pose is unmistakable. I would know it anywhere, that look, that pulling away, that hand upraised to
keep off scrutiny. It is a hand that will build a wall of
secrets, that will run across the world to look for a hiding
spot, that will see every last hope crumble around it and
never concede defeat, never say: it is enough.

Around me, night has fallen. Under this comforting
blanket of dark I have climbed to the watch spot on the
uppermost deck. There is a narrow crawl space here, a thin
brace of bars separating me from the world of nothingness
that I cannot see.

I have left the computer in my stateroom, but the head-
lines are still looping crazy circles through my brain. They
taunt me with all they say, and madden me with all they do
not. The relationship of Rupert Payne Jr. and Helena Finn

waltzed across the big tabloids, though the two seemed to do all they could to avoid the limelight. Whispered talks of marriage began to surface, all adamantly denied by the House of Payne.

And then the couple eloped. The scandal monopolized a month's worth of gossip columns, and the buzz contained little else. But Rupert and Helena were long gone, having left immediately on a whirlwind honeymoon tour of Asia.

Until disaster struck. Here, oddly, the news reports evaporate. At this, my most desperate point of interest, I could find only two or three online journals containing the bare facts. But even those facts shake the foundation of my world.

On a mild September morning, the cleaning staff at the Fitzroy-Balmoral in Kuala Lumpur entered the penthouse/honeymoon suite to find the young bridegroom facedown in the decorative koi pool.

Dead by drowning.

Of the new bride there was no sign, and some of the magazines speculated on the connection. Could she have murdered her husband? Why else would she make such a sudden—and suspicious—departure? Didn't she stand to inherit the Payne fortune after the hastily thrown-together nuptials?

Much was left unclear. But a few things are perfectly obvious to me now:

My father is dead.

My mother fled the scene rather than allow herself to be questioned. I know there is no way she could have been responsible for his death. But still she ran.

And then someone—someone with a long arm and a successful reach—hushed up almost all mention of the incident. It is almost as if the whole thing had never happened.

Almost as if my parents had never met at all.

I hang my head and, for long moments, sob out my longing for my father, for all that is left of him now—his memory. I let myself feel, really feel the pain, let it wash through me until there is nothing left but the sound of waves lapping against the side of the vessel and the grinding of the ship's motor.

At last I am spent. Alone in the dark, I drink in the silence like strong tea. I wonder if this is how Mama felt, so trapped that she needed to find a place where she could not see or be seen. Did being half-dead make it easier for her to live? Did she really think this was the better choice?

Because this is a choice I would never make. I am not at home in the darkness.

I think back to the cell where I grew up, and the comforting glow still hangs around it in my mind's eye—that knowing every step and corner of a place, that intimate bonding that comes from a life well lived and a small world fully explored.

But over it still drapes the shadow of hidden things,

the gloom of secrets. It was still a prison. I have spent my life in the dark; now I am ready to step into the light.

In the distance, the sun cracks the horizon and begins to drive its pale wedge of light into the world. As I watch, the darkness is diluted, so that without realizing it I am beginning to see things around me—my hands, my knees, the bars on my lookout post, the deck of the ship far below, the tossing waves that support me on this final journey.

I turn my face into the early sun. And there, shadowed against the far horizon, I see a sight that makes me catch my breath.

It is far off still, so far that it's only a shadowed bulk in the pale almost-light. But it is there. A bar of land on the horizon.

My destination.

America.

Without thinking I reach up and clutch the railing next to me, knuckles white with tension. I feel a tear trickle down my cheek. I am almost there.

And the girl inside me glances back over her shoulder at the cell she has left behind, that world shrouded in darkness that she has pushed through and survived. It was far from perfect, that life of my childhood. For better or worse it did make me into who I am, and for this I can never fault it.

But never again will I belong to that world.

And more. Never again will I choose darkness when

there can be light. Never again will I hide when there is a chance to fling wide my arms and *know*. Never again will I hold myself captive to the power of secrets.

In all these things, though perhaps without meaning to, Mama has taught me well.

40

At breakfast that morning, the captain eats his oatmeal in silence, his chin drooping down toward his dish, his eyes focused on nothing. This is so unusual that after the meal I trail him back to his stateroom and stand awkwardly by the door. After a few minutes, he looks up and sees me there. He cracks a wan smile.

"Luchi, my girl," he says.

"Captain, something's not right with you. What's going on?"

"Right?" he says, too quickly. "Of course everything's all right. Peachy keen it is, right as rain, good as—" He breaks off and stands suddenly, frowning at the ground. Then he heaves a full-body sigh and throws himself into an armchair. He waves his arm at me and I step inside and sit on the floor, leaning against the end of the bed.

"It's this confounded journey," he says, "coming to an end and all that. It had to end sometime, right? But now it really is. We'll be in Oakland by tomorrow nightfall. And all this, us, you—it's all going to be gone. It's like"—he swallows, and his words are so low I can barely hear them, as he turns his head away from me—"it's like Mandy, like losing her all over again."

And what can I say to that? He is right, in a sense, but there is nothing I can do to make things better. Truthfully, I'm feeling a little that way myself. I'm leaving something sure, something I understand, and stepping out into the unknown. Again. And yet—isn't that what got me here to begin with?

"Sometimes," I whisper, "all we can do is take that step. Even if we have to leave a little bit of ourselves behind with those we love." I'm talking to myself, and I've almost forgotten the captain's in the room until he moves in his chair and lifts his head. Heat grows in my cheeks, but to my surprise he smiles.

He doesn't say anything, though, just gives me that smile, then turns his head to the window. We sit there, he and I, while long minutes spool out and the boat chugs slowly forward, ever forward.

Then the captain shakes himself and turns back toward me. His eyes are clear again, his gaze strong. He speaks as though my last words were just a moment ago. "Aw, girlie, and don't you know a thing or two about loss and striking out for the great unknown? I guess if you're not moping around and giving up, I've got no excuse to either, do I?"

That wasn't what I meant at all, and I open my mouth to say so, but he silences me with a wave. "Not another word," he says, pulling fingers across his lips. "Zip zip, it's over. I've been an insufferable bum, wallowing over a past I can't undo. Well, no more of that. It's not that I won't miss Mandy, but—" He seems to be searching for the right thing to say. "But I guess that's the biggest thing I've seen from having you around. You're so much like her, you know. She wasn't nobody's quitter. If tough times came her way, she'd hit 'em head-on and keep going. I guess she'd want her old man to do the same."

The captain crosses the room, reaches down, and I lift up my hand to let him pull me to my feet. "Thank you for helping me remember that," he says.

I don't know what to say, but in the next breath, the captain's moved on to other subjects. "So—America, huh? How do you feel? First time on home soil and all that. Nervous? Excited?"

I look at the floor. "Both."

"I wish I could be there for your first impressions, but there's a truckload of paperwork and red tape I gotta clear to get my baby"—he waves his hand around him to indicate the ship—"into port. You'll want to make sure your papers are all in order, though. Those immigration dogs are fierce."

A slow trickle of ice water starts in my chest. "Papers?"

Captain Jensen eyes me. "Sure—passport, birth certificate, all that good stuff. You—of course, you do have those things, right?"

My mind races. Do I?

I dash out of the room and into the hall. The captain follows at my heels. In my stateroom, I pull out my tea box with trembling hands. A passport—yes. In the name of Helena Finn, age twenty-one when it was issued sixteen years ago. A birth certificate—yes. In Thai, smudged and crumpled and signed with a hand-made seal.

Captain Jensen sinks down onto my bed, his face melting like wax. "Oh, child," he whispers, and then, "Of course. It's obvious, really. And why would you? How could you? But oh—I should have thought of it. What are we going to do?"

The room is silent as the seconds of my life tick by, and I start to wonder if this whole journey was in vain, if I will arrive at my destination only to find the doors locked and barred. And what will happen to me then? Where will I go?

Forward, I tell myself.

Whatever happens, wherever I go, let it be forward.

41

The ship makes landfall in the early morning. A shiny red bridge gleams off to our rear, glowing like an ember in the midmorning sun. Just ahead is the hulking gray mass of buildings and machinery that is the port of Oakland, California. It is the first of July, and with the new month will begin my new life.

It took us hours to accept that there was not much to be done about my papers. But Captain Jensen has written me a notarized letter that he says I am to present along with the documents I have. The letter is full of big words and fancy sayings, and I know these are not altogether true. He is not a longtime family friend who knew my mama well and was entrusted by her to take care of me. But in some ways, these words are truer than the truth.

I hope they will be enough.

We have talked about my plans from here. I have brushed up on my map studies and found that Boston is not an easy walk from California. It is, in fact, a distance almost as great as the one I have just traveled. My grandmother's website has also provided me with her phone number, and I have promised the captain that I will call her as soon as I am safely in the country. He will be in California for only a few days' stopover, but he has arranged for me to stay in a hotel near the port until my plans are finalized. He cannot speak to the immigration people with me—he has his ship to see to, after all—but he will meet up with me when I am allowed to leave the ship and officially enter the country.

Once again it hits me how grateful I am for his care, this kind, gruff man who has turned all my rags into finery and given my life a tinge of magic. But now the clock is striking midnight, and even he cannot say what is up ahead for me.

It's time to say good-bye.

I turn to the captain, and he leans forward and pulls me into an awkward hug.

"You just hang tight in there, you hear?" he says. "You're stronger than you think—yup, I mean that! You are quite something, my girl. And you don't need a graying old sea captain like me to tell you that. You're made of the right stuff, Luchi Finn." He leans back and holds my chin in his hand, looks me right in the eye. "You can do anything you set your mind to."

I hold his look, and I don't reach up to wipe away the tears that are pouring down my cheeks, because as long as I'm fixed on the old captain's eyes, I believe him.

But once I'm alone in my room, carrying case on the

floor stuffed with the new things I've accumulated during my sea trip, I'm less sure. The passengers are each to wait in their quarters as the officials make the rounds, checking up on every one of us in turn.

So silent, in this big empty stateroom. So much quiet time for thinking. So many spaces for fear to creep up and slide cold fingers down my back.

And the hours.

Crawl.

By.

I think I could go crazy with this waiting, but finally there's a rap at my door and two stiff, well-pressed men stride in. Their presence eats up all the air in the room, and I feel myself shrinking even smaller as my heart hammers loud in my chest. I think of Mama's nameless terror, how she tried so desperately to stay hidden, to keep herself—and me—out of sight. Aren't these just the type of men she would have hidden from?

The paperwork shakes in my hand. Can I really do this?

Do I have any other choice?

"Luchi Ann Finn," the front man barks out, reading from the passenger list in his hand.

I swallow. I can do this. Taking a deep breath, I stand and hold out my papers. Mama's passport is on top, and the man opens it with a bored look on his face. Mama's face looks out from her picture, fragile and innocent.

She has no idea that she is being betrayed by her own daughter.

I feel my lunch rising in my throat. What have I done?

The official is frowning at the passport, comparing it against his list, then he looks back at me. "What is this?" he snaps. He shuffles through my papers, gapes at the Thai document. "The name's not even the same. This isn't you. You're a kid, for Pete's sake. What's going on here?" Then he settles on the captain's letter, reads it through, stops and looks me up and down. He holds the paper to his nose, studying the raised seal of the notary's stamp. He reads it through again, leans in and exchanges a few words with his partner, whose dark brows are pulled together in a scowl. "Man oh man, why do I always get the head cases? You'll need to wait here while we look into this."

My hands feel icy cold. I'm moving through a frozen river; I shuffle unsteadily back across the room and collapse into a chair. The two men step out into the hallway and I can hear the stomp of feet as someone else arrives. I can barely see them through the half-opened door, hunched over my papers, whispering and conferring and sneaking suspicious looks in my direction. Snippets of their conversation float over to me: . . . *send her back?* . . . *obvious she is related* . . . *anyone read this language?* . . . *call to dig up some more info* . . .

What have I set into motion? What will be my punishment for breaking my vow of secrecy? I remember again Mama's final words, urging me to keep the promises I'd made. To keep her secrets. My chin sinks onto my chest.

Outside the door there are clicks and mutters, as someone speaks into a phone. Investigating my right to exist? My right to enter the country? My relationship to Mama?

It's all too much, and I can't help but imagine the worst. It seems like the most reasonable thing to do, under the circumstances.

Finally the first official pushes back into the room and strides toward me. His brows are knit together and his mouth is turned down as I scramble to my feet. He holds out Mama's passport and my papers. "Frankly, Miss Finn, I don't know what to make of you. But it's out of my hands now." He's tapping his finger on the form where I have written the name of the hotel the captain reserved for me. "This where you'll be staying?"

I nod, biting down on a question that I can't bring myself to ask. Were the papers enough, then? Have I made it through?

My wondering is short-lived.

"I'm afraid you'll need to stay put for just a little longer. Our agents will accompany you to your hotel, but you'll be confined to your room until further notice. There's no doubt of your citizenship, but there was a flag out on your mother's name, so we need to follow procedure on this. I'm sure you can understand."

Confined to my room? For how long? And . . . a flag on Mama's name? All my worst fears rise in my throat like bile. I have never felt more alone in my life.

"Wait," I whisper. "I would like to speak with my grand-mother. Mrs. Regina Finn. From Brookline."

She'll be able to help me. She'll know what to do.

The man smirks. "Oh, you'll be speaking to her, all right. We've got people calling her up already. And, of course, the main interested party has already been noti-fied, Mr. Rupert God-Almighty Payne." He grunts. "How that man thinks he can just pull on the strings and expect everyone to do his bidding, I'll never know. But everyone does, so there's no way I'm going to question it."

Still shaking his head, he stalks out of the room, leav-ing me with two uniformed guards who step silently up in his wake.

The last piece of the puzzle slides into place. Mr. Rupert Payne Sr. My father's father. This must be the person who kept all the news details quiet. So this must also be the monster man Mama was so afraid of.

And he knows I am here.

I have no breath. I have no thoughts. My mind is empty and hollow as I turn and follow these strangers who are leading me away.

To meet the man my mother spent a lifetime in prison to avoid.

42

The morning wind swells the water as I step off the gangplank and onto firm ground. After being on the ship for so long, the land seems to quiver and quake, and I grab a post to steady myself. With the guards beside me, though, there is little time for noticing my surroundings, only a terrible constant forward motion.

My legs nearly buckle at the sight of Captain Jensen waiting just ahead. He rushes up to me but is cut short when my two very tall, very wide escorts block his way. They stand on either side of me and glower at him.

"What's going on here?" the captain yelps.

I open my mouth to explain, but the guards don't stop to talk. They each grab one of my arms and begin to move me away. My carrying case knocks painfully behind me. Finally one of the guards picks it up while the second continues to herd me along.

The captain, meanwhile, starts yelling and chases around to place his small frame in our path. "Whoa! Geeyup, boys, hold it right there. What exactly do you think you're doing? This girl is my charge and I am looking out for her. You aren't taking her nowhere, not any single where. You just put her down right now."

The first man drops my bag and reaches toward a holster on his hip, but the second puts a hand on his arm as if to quiet him. "Look here," he says, whipping out his wallet and flashing a badge in the captain's face. "See? We don't want no trouble. We've got our orders: Escort this young lady to her hotel room, no stops and no interruptions. Guard her there until the interested parties arrive and the all clear is given. She won't be harmed, but you'll understand that procedure's got to be followed."

The captain puffs up his chest like a blowfish. "Procedure can go hang itself!" he screeches. "This girl is a minor, and she's in my care, and I have the legal documents to prove it. Anywhere she goes, I'm going, too. Is that clear?"

The guards stare down at this diminutive man in the oversized uniform who is snarling at them like a cat facing two bulldogs. They exchange glances, and the first one shrugs. "Suit yourself. Boss didn't say nothing about having no guests. Just see that you both keep up. And no dawdling!"

And with that I am moving again, following the guards across shiny wide-open spaces and up a magical moving staircase that nips at my toes when I don't step fast enough; into the back of a car with dark tinted windows that feels like the warm inside of a cell; then out again, into the sunshine, and in the front lobby of a building so tall I get dizzy searching for the top.

I am given a thick plastic card, which I am told is a key. I step into a tiny room with no windows. The silvery doors slide shut and numbers start to flash on an electronic display, climbing higher and higher. My stomach turns somersaults. My ears feel stuffed with cotton. I want to scream as I grab the captain's hand. "What's going on?" No one acts like anything unusual is happening.

The captain looks at me, surprised; then his eyes soften. "There, there," he says. "Of course you haven't been in an elevator before. It's for going up—real fast. Wait'll you get out. You'll see. Up on the thirty-fourth floor, you are." At his words, a bell dings and the doors slide open. In a trance, I move to the window, where my stomach lurches. Nothing— not the roof of the prison or the top of Golden Mount that day with Chaluay—nothing could have prepared me for this sight. The whole world is distance. There is water and grass and trees and buildings—and they are all the size of beetles.

I could stand and stare all day at this make-believe world out the windows, but one of the guards makes an angry noise in his throat. I move quickly away and find the room number I was given. The captain shows me how to slide my card through a slot, and to wait until a tiny light shines green before opening up the door.

My eyes fill with tears. This world is even stranger than the one I left behind in Bangkok. How will I navigate it alone?

I know the captain can't stay, much as he wishes to. He helps me to get settled, answers all my questions, and reassures me that he won't leave until he is sure all is well with my situation. But I refuse. He has a ship to care for, a ship the size of a small village. He has goods and crew and paperwork all awaiting his return. His freighter must take to the sea again in two days, after all.

We both know I'm right, but it doesn't make this parting any easier. With everything said that can be said, Captain Jensen stands awkwardly in the doorway, scuffing one shoe over the other. Then he looks up and harrumphs. "Come here, my girl," he says, and opens his arms wide.

My breath catches in my throat, and then—I topple into his hug. He's no bigger than I am, but his arms are tough and wiry, and I can hear the wheezing breath in his chest. Mama's and Bibi's, those are the only arms that have held me before now. This thought hangs on me and almost eclipses the moment. Almost. Because nothing can take away the fact that this gruff old man has become, over the course of a few weeks, someone I will never forget.

"Ah, you dear thing, won't you always have a place of honor in this old seafaring man's heart," he mutters into my hair.

I squeeze him harder and I whisper into his shoulder, "Good-bye." It's all I can say, choked up as I am, but this word I haven't spoken in months, this word I swore I would never say again, is my gift to him, an attempt at thanks, a sign of this new me that he has helped create.

And as the door closes behind him, it occurs to me that I have spent the last few weeks trying to learn about the father I never knew, when all along someone else was slowly slipping into that empty spot in my heart. And filling it up completely.

I look at the paper the captain left me with his address, and I hope that we will meet again someday. I smile when I think that for every loss there is a gain, for every lock there is a key. And for every dark question there is an answer waiting to be found.

If I can only keep looking for it.

43

Hours pass. Before he left, the captain set up the laptop computer he'd insisted I take with me, so that I can access the Internet here in the hotel room. When I turn the machine on, I smile to see that Kiet has replied to my e-mail. He is well, but life as a monk does not give him much time to write.

It occurs to me that the ideal monk may not spend much time in an Internet café composing e-mails to girls in foreign countries. But I am glad that this monk values our friendship enough to make it happen. I busy myself writing him back and this, too, helps the time creep forward. It also fills a warm place in my chest. If I close my eyes, for a moment I can almost feel I'm back in the car with Kiet, speeding down the highway with the rain streaming in the windows.

It feels so much more real than this strange new reality.

When my eyes hurt from looking at the computer screen, I explore my new surroundings. The room is almost twice the size of Chaluay's whole apartment in Bangkok. One giant bed sprawls along the wall, and there is a separate space with armchairs and a low table, and even a television. In the late afternoon the telephone rings and a voice asks me what I would like to eat. I fumble through a printed menu as instructed, but the fancy curly writing sounds nothing like real food.

Cheeks blazing, I call out the first thing my gaze falls on, which is a cheeseburger and fries. The name is familiar from my reading on the ship but here, now, in this wide white room with big shiny windows and soft covered floors, it is just another part of the wrongness, another part of this world where I do not fit. When the dish finally arrives I look for long minutes at the round circles of bread, the patty of meat with melted cheese and some vegetables. I try a french fry. It is crispy and delicious, but even this does not satisfy my real hunger, my need for the known.

I attack my plate with fork and knife, cut the bread and meat and fries into small pieces and toss them all together. It is only a little like stir-fry, and the flavors are all wrong, but it fills something deep inside me. This place holds so much that is strange, so much that is new. But inside, I am still me. I can still touch this world and make it into something I can understand.

And so I wait.

And wait.

And wait, as the hours tick by and the afternoon slides into night. I read and I watch stupid people on television fall around while invisible ghosts laugh and laugh, but I cannot understand what they are laughing at because none of the falling or tripping or hurting seems to be funny.

It's full dark out now. My eyes feel like lead. I will rest them just for a few minutes.

I am awakened by a rapping on the door. Outside my window there is a clear, light sky and, from somewhere far away, the sound of early-morning birdsong. Has the whole night passed so quickly, in one big gulp? I wonder who is at the door, though I am in no shape to see anyone at all. I rush to the bathroom.

This tiny chamber terrifies me—it's small and hot and breathy; filled, everywhere I look, with images of *me*. I remember the postcard-sized mirror in its blue plastic frame that hung on our cell wall. How I loved that silvery reflection when I was young! It was like having a friend who was always just my age. But this room holds three reflections, big and tall and wide, all showing the same thing: this girl, this wide-eyed, terror-struck girl with electric hair and wrinkled clothes—who is she? Do I even know who I am becoming?

I take a deep breath, lift my head, and lock eyes with my own reflection. It doesn't matter who I was or who I will someday be. Right now, I am myself. That's all that matters.

The knocking at the door starts again, still tentative but a little more insistent. The person at the door is not going to go away. A little water helps to smooth my hair and clean the crusts out of my eyes. My shirt and shorts look slept in and nowhere near presentable, but it will have to do.

I step back into the room, move to the door, and pull it open.

And my breath catches in my throat.

It's her—Regina Finn.

My grandmother.

She looks a lot like her picture on the web page, only a little older and more wrinkled. If I am stunned to silence, it's nothing compared to the look on her face. She has seen a ghost, a whole house full of ghosts, alive and walking toward her. She goes pale green, then white, then bright pink. A plastic bag falls from one hand and a leather purse slides off the other arm. She is frozen, arms outstretched like an old leafless tree.

She seems to have lost all ability to speak, too, and the guards are starting to look awkwardly in our direction, so I squat down and pick up the bag and the purse. Then I let a slow smile fill my face.

"Grandmother," I say.

It is the most beautiful word in the whole world.

44

I turn from the entryway and step into the room. She walks behind me, moves inside, and lets me shut the door behind her. But she's still silent as an old blackwood, and her gaze sticks to me like sap. I place the bags on the table and wave her toward one of the chairs. She falls into it without even looking once behind her. She devours me with her eyes.

"Grandmother," I say again.

"Yes," she whispers finally, and that word seems to break her trance. Suddenly her eyes are full of tears, and the tears are spilling down her face so that in seconds it's wet, dripping wet, and I'm starting to get worried. I don't know what to do, so I jump up and grab some tissues from the bathroom. I stuff them in her hand and she buries her face in them, sobbing and hiccuping a little.

"I'm sorry," she says. "I'm so sorry, it's just that you—you're so much—so—so much like your—like your mother. She's gone, isn't she?" And she hardly waits for my nod before she buries her head in her hands and weeps again.

I know about tears, how good they can be for a person. Mama always waited until I was asleep before she let the really big tears come, but they woke me up every time. I would lie with my back turned away from her, thinking that at any time I could turn around, ever so slightly, and she would see me awake—and then what? For some reason she was ashamed of her weeping, but she shouldn't have been. She would cry noisy tears of rage and despair, and slowly the sobs would roll up inside each other, would nestle into the folds of her body, would become softer and rounder, like rocking, like comfort. Like healing.

The next morning, she always woke up with red eyes but a soft smile, like she'd wrestled with an angel and won herself a few moments of peace.

So I let my grandmother cry now, and I sit quietly next to her, not saying anything, not moving a muscle, until I recognize the comfort sobs. Then I do what I was never able to do for Mama: I lean over, wrap my arms around her, and place my head on her shoulder.

We stay like that for a while, until all her tears are gone and she pulls away with an embarrassed smile. "Thank you," she whispers. "I suppose I had to get that out of my system, but—oh! You!" Her eyes mist up and for a second I think she's going to start all over again, but she doesn't. "Look at you—tell me everything about yourself! I suppose Rupert—"

"My father," I say quickly. There are two Ruperts, after all, and I don't want to mix them up. "I never knew him. He died."

"Yes," she says. "But you—"

"I only found out about him recently. Mama was . . . secretive."

"But how—where have you been all these years? Why did she never . . ."

I reach into my pocket and fish out a very creased, very worn piece of paper, almost translucent now from so much handling. I put it on the table in front of her, and I can see from her face that she recognizes it instantly.

"My letter. She got it."

"She was afraid," I say quickly. "I—I still don't know exactly why. I don't understand everything. But she was in prison. They arrested her going into Thailand. That's where I was born. Where I grew up. In the prison."

My grandmother's eyes widen with horror. "No!"

I nod, then I smile. "Come," I say. "Let me show you." I reach out my hand for hers and she takes it, and we stand up together—and now we're in my cell, on the inside, in the room that was my life. Words bubble up and out of me like magic, like mystery, like big wide strokes of paint sweeping across the mind's canvas. I show her my cot and the sums I scratched on the walls, my well-loved books and my skillful tutors. I show her science and math, spelling and languages, stories and cuddles and a sort of crazy personalized attention that somehow, despite what it lacked, gave me everything I needed to become who I am. I introduce her to Bibi and Isra, Chief Warden Kanya, and even grouchy Jeanne.

And I give her Mama. I give her the tall, slender

woman who crooned her toddler to sleep every night; the madcap dance teacher who got us doing the rumba at midnight when the fancy struck her; the sad, lonely mother who cried herself to sleep but kept her back strong so that I wouldn't worry. I give it all to her, big and little, good and bad, and in this way the day slips by. Food comes, or maybe it doesn't. We are not there. We are just outside of Chiang Mai, in a tiny up-country prison, reclaiming thirteen lost years, one memory at a time.

It is the most wonderful of all days. My grandmother and I fit like we are cut from the same blanket. She eats up all my stories, and her questions draw out memories I'd forgotten I had, little things Mama said, stories and songs and nonsense words that make us both roll around with shared laughter. It's like having a little of Mama back.

As we sit in the dark room that night, eating my newest favorite food—pancakes with little button-sized berryfruits and pillows of whipped cream—I get up and walk to my bag. I reach to the very bottom, pull out a mass of dirty bundled cloth, and carry it to where she is sitting. The cloth strips come off easily, with all the wear this bundle's gotten, and my grandmother's eyes fill again as she looks at the urn. She knows right away what it is.

"Thank you," she says. "You brought your mama home to me. Thank you for that, dear child. Do you know that I felt it when she went? I truly did. But I never imagined she left someone behind—some bit of her, still in the world. And now you're here, with me."

"Grandmother," I say, because I can't seem to stop

thinking it, and the word just slips out of my mouth some-times without trying.

Her lips curve up into an amused smile. "Nana," she says. "It's always been 'Nana' on my side of the family."

"Nana," I say, trying it out. I haven't heard the term before, but it fits her. It's soft and sturdy, with no sharp edges. It's just right. "Nana."

She sets the urn carefully on the table. The unfinished brown clay looks dull and foreign on the gleaming glass countertop, like a plant that's been transposed into the wrong kind of soil. But this isn't the end of Mama's jour-ney. She's not all the way home yet.

"Home," I say. "Do you still live in Brookline, where Mama grew up?"

"Yes! Oh, yes! And I can't wait to take you there. In fact—" She looks at her watch. "No, I suppose it's too late to get tickets for tonight. But we should plan to fly out first thing in the morning."

Then I remember something. "The man at the border said . . ." My mouth is suddenly dry, and I wonder how all the comfort and love of the past few hours could have crowded something so important out of my head. "He is coming."

Nana's head snaps up. "What?"

"Ru—" I shake my head. I can't say his name, but I don't have to. She hisses like an angry snake and leaps to her feet. My hands start to tremble. "They said his name was put in Mama's file; she was flagged as a person of interest.

They called him at the same time as you. They said—I couldn't leave here—until . . ."

The soft old woman is gone; in her place is a roaring monsoon. Nana yanks the door open and darts out into the hall. I can hear her voice, raised and sharp, and the guards' deep bass counterpoint. I sink lower in my chair. Somehow, I know what's coming. There was a look on that guard's face when he told me who was in charge.

And it wasn't my grandmother.

Sure enough, when she comes back into the room, her shoulders are drooping. "They won't let you leave," she says in a near whisper. "I don't know how he thinks he can still—"

Suddenly I can't bear the suspense any longer. I rush to her and drop to my knees by her chair. "Please, tell me everything," I say. "Who is this man, and why was Mama so afraid of him? What did he do to her?" What, I think to myself, would be so horrible that she would choose a life in prison over facing him again?

Nana sighs. She closes her eyes and falls against the back of her chair like an empty coat. "Old man Payne is the meanest son of a gun you'll ever find. He built Payne Industries up from nothing to a billion-dollar company before he was twenty-five. Whatever he set his eye on, he got. That's the word on the street, and that's been my experience, too. He's made himself into one of the most powerful men on the East Coast, and, of course, he had great plans for his only son, Rupert Jr."

A shudder ripples through me. Without thinking I sit back into a squat, hugging my knees tightly against my chest.

"But that boy was nothing like him. He was . . ." She searches for the right word, then waves a hand as if to pull it out of the air. "Good. He was a good boy. Helena met him at a club when she was nineteen. She'd gone out with a couple of girlfriends, and I don't know how it happened, but they ended up getting to know each other. He came by the house a few times—quiet, well mannered, nicely dressed. He didn't use his real name. Rupert Ray, he called himself—that was his middle name. Didn't like the attention that came with the full version." Her mouth twisted. "Not that I can blame him.

"In any case, time passed and eventually things started getting serious between them, and it was then he told her who he was. Of course, she didn't care, but there was more to it than that. Payne's people kept tabs on his son, and he finally caught on that this was more than some little fling. Payne warned his son to drop your mother and move on."

"Why?" I ask. "Why did he dislike her so much?"

Nana shrugs. "Many things, I suppose. Not highly placed enough. Not rich enough. Not well-connected enough. Not his choice. In any case, Rupert ignored his father, and next thing we know, Helena disappears."

I gasp. "What happened to her?"

Nana's eyes cast down to her lap. "I don't know. She would never tell. She was gone for four days, but after the second night Rupert came to the house. He thought she'd been ignoring his calls, and when he found out she was missing, he was livid. I've never seen a man so angry. He let us know his father had to be involved, and he swore he would get her back to us." She shakes her head, looking suddenly very old. "He did, too. But she was never the same. She came back with eyes as big as oceans and hands that wouldn't stop shaking. Anytime anyone around her moved a hand too quickly—for any reason at all—she would fly out of her chair and be halfway across the room before she even knew what she was doing. She would wake up at night screaming and whimpering. It was horrible."

"Was she hurt?" I whisper. "Did he hurt her?"

"No. There were no marks on her body, nothing. But she was broken, all the same."

Broken. How well that word describes Mama! And how I wish I'd known all of this sooner. I could have helped her. I know I could have.

"We all tried to help," says Nana, as if she's reading my mind. "She wouldn't let us go to the police—what good would it have done anyway, with so many of them in Payne's pocket? And over time, things did get better. Of course she wanted nothing to do with Rupert, wouldn't take his calls, begged us not to let him anywhere near the house. But he kept coming, kept leaving her flowers, sending her books with notes scrawled into the flyleaf." She wipes away a tear. "He really loved her. I read in the papers that he had broken ties with his father, disowned him publicly and denounced him for corruption. It was a huge scandal." Her mouth twists. "Or it should have been, except it wasn't. The newspapers were all ablaze for, oh, one day. Then, suddenly, the whole thing disappeared. Poof! Not a whisper on the web, in print, on TV, nothing. It's like it never happened. He has connections in high places, that old man."

"So what happened then?"

"Rupert won her over, eventually. She loved him as much as he did her, you see. And finally he broke through her fear and got her to believe that there was hope for a happy ending."

"They ran away," I whisper.

"Yes. She wasn't supposed to tell me—Rupert didn't want to risk word getting to his father. But she left me a letter." She reaches down to touch her skirt pocket, and I wonder if maybe she carries it with her wherever she goes. It wouldn't surprise me. "I was devastated at first—but I understood. She loved him. And—well, I just never thought things would end the way they did. He was a good boy. But he wasn't perfect. He had some terrible flaws of his own."

I think about the end of the story, my father's sad end. "I read on the computer about what happened," I say.

Nana nods. "Payne hushed most of that up, too. But his contacts aren't as strong abroad, so some word got out and stayed out. I didn't know then what Rupert was into, though we found out more details later, and I can't say I was surprised when we did—I can't imagine growing up with a father like that! And his mother died so young." She sighs. "But that was the last I heard; after his death Helena just disappeared. I never thought it would all end like that."

We bow our heads, then I reach up and wipe my eyes. "No," I say. "That wasn't her end—don't you see? In some strange way, she got what she wanted. She was—" And I see this with a sudden, shocking clarity. "Happy. Most of the time, she really was happy there. In prison. In her own way, she was. They were good to us. They took care of us. I think—with the bars and the guards—I think she felt safe."

Nana is crying again, but a sudden noise at the door catches our attention.

Footsteps. Raised voices. And then a loud, thunderous knock.

"Oh, no," Nana whispers. "He's here."

45

It's all happening too quickly. What can we do? There's no escape. We are imprisoned here as surely as I ever was on the inside.

The pounding at the door comes again, and I can hear the guard's voice: "It's quite late, sir. Ms. Finn might well be sleeping."

The return voice is low with a cold fury. "She will not be sleeping for long. And if you wish to retain your employment, I suggest you restrict your opinion to matters which concern you."

"Yes sir, Mr. Payne," comes the reply, and feet shuffle away from the door as the pounding starts up again.

So this is it. I am to meet for myself the source of that haze of fear in my mother's eyes, that terror she danced with by day and cowered from by night. Rupert Payne Sr. is standing like the devil on my doorstep. "Stay back," Nana whispers, starting to get up. "I'll go deal with him."

But I get to my feet first, put a hand on her arm. "No," I say. "I have to do this. For Mama. I need to do this."

She looks deep into my eyes, then nods. "He can't hurt you," she says. "He won't hurt you. I'm here. The guards are here. We'll all stand up to him together."

I smile and squeeze her hand, but as I move toward the door that is now rattling on its hinges with the force of the blows, I've never been less sure of anything in my life. Breathing slowly and deliberately, trying not to sink into the fear my mind is screaming out, I unlatch the door. And swing it open.

Rupert Payne Sr. leaps into the room like he has a rocket strapped to his back. He grabs my arms with both hands, then looks me up and down. His face goes a darker shade of red. He shoves me to the side with a curse. "Out of the way, child. Where is she? Where is that . . . Helena Finn!" he bellows. "Where are you? Didn't I warn you? Didn't I tell you what would happen?"

The storm of fury has clearly been building for a long time, because he doesn't seem to take in his surroundings. He seems lost in the moment as he rants and raves out his hatred for my mother, calls her every name he can think of.

And I smile.

It's a slow smile, but it starts right in my core and grows out with a spreading warmth. Because he didn't win. He didn't. My mother—my weak, terrified, fear-driven mother—spent her life battling this monster. And she won.

A dubious victory, perhaps. But she was never beaten. He never got her.

And he won't get me, either. I push off from the wall where I've been huddled and move into his line of vision. "Stop!" I yell, and to my surprise, he does.

He blinks and looks at me. "Who are you?" he asks.

"I'm Luchi Finn, Helena's daughter."

At her name, he starts up again. "Where is she? I told her—"

But I cut him off. "She's dead." And I watch with satisfaction as the blow lands.

"What? But the border official said—" He glowers at me. "You're lying. I had a flag on her name—they called me because she had returned."

"Then your spies don't have their facts right," says Nana, speaking up for the first time and coming to put her arm around my shoulder. "If you're looking for my Helena, here she is." She's holding the urn in her arms, and for a second I'm afraid she'll shove it at him, but instead she holds it tight to her chest.

Payne looks at Nana, then at me, then down at the urn. Then—he crumples. He drops like a broken branch that's been holding up a mountain and has finally collapsed under the strain. He folds in on himself and falls to the ground in front of us, gasping like a fish.

What's he doing? I look over at Nana. She grabs my arm with her free hand, and that's when I know it for sure—though I still can't believe it.

Rupert Payne Sr. is lying at our feet, crying his eyes out.

We stand and watch him, and it's nothing like it was with Nana earlier, because I'm still angry with him, so angry, and I don't want to let him get to that comfort stage. So I squat down next to him and lean in to his face. "What are you doing?" I ask. "It's not enough that you killed her, now that she's dead you can't take it?"

He shakes his head, his eyes wild, his wrinkled jowls swaying. "It's not like that," he rasps. "You don't understand how it's been. This rage . . ." He takes a long breath. "This rage is all I have lived for, all that has kept me going for the last fifteen years. It's my backbone. It's been my life! And now—by God, now I hardly know why it started." He looks up, searching Nana's face. "Why did I drive him away? Why did I hate her so much? I think . . . I think maybe I thought that if I could get her back, if I hated her enough, I could somehow turn back time, bring *him* back. If I could get revenge on her, I could make up for his loss."

I look at him. He's so small, and the hate rises in me like a living thing.

"Well, I'm here now," I spit out. "I'm her daughter. You can take your revenge on me in her place."

Nana sucks in her breath and squeezes my arm in an iron grip, but he just shakes his head and rises to his feet. "Will you get me some water?"

It's delivered more as a statement than as a question and, shaking her head, Nana trundles off to the bathroom. Payne stands there rocking slightly, looking at me and shaking his head. And that's when I know that it's over—this reign of terror, this giant of a man. He tried to break my mother, but somehow, with her silence and her disappearance and her unwillingness to give in, she broke him. He'll never be what he was.

And, quite likely, the world will be a better place.

46

There is a lot of telling after this, so many questions and answers and tears and heartbreak. So many bridges to mend. So many webs to untangle.

Old Payne—I still won't call him my grandfather—in his new broken state, having released his long-held rage, surprises us by becoming a rational, tolerable person.

"I'm not going anywhere," he tells us. "You're family now, the only family I have left. I'm sitting right here until we figure out what's going to happen next." And so we talk. He and Nana grudgingly find they have more in common than they'd expected, especially when food is called for and their tastes agree.

And over plates of fruit and saltines and caviar and pâté, we talk. The story builds slowly, like the old television on the guards' table outside my cell, where you have to tune it so carefully, a nudge of the dial here, a bump of the knob there, twisting and turning and all the while the image is getting clearer and sharper until all of a sudden you have it: a whole image, a picture, a tale that unfolds as real as real life. This is the story that my mother's mother and my father's father weave their separate facts together to reveal.

The story of a rich, entitled young man who had everything but wanted only to be seen for who he really was. The story of a young girl who met a stranger at a bar and found her soul mate. These two shared a passion so deep that nothing, no impossibility seemed too great. They only wanted each other. And when society didn't agree, they left—flew around the world in search of that peace they were denied at home.

The peace they would never find.

For there was a fatal flaw in their perfect world, a deadly white powder that ultimately would bring about their destruction. It is unclear how far back the drug use had started, but young Rupert had a weakness that could not be controlled. He had tried to break the habit so many times, had promised his young bride he would never go near the stuff again.

"Helena was straight-edge as they come," Nana whispers. "She didn't even drink alcohol—tried it once at seventeen and swore never to touch it again. Her father—my husband—he was an alcoholic. We divorced when she was seven, but Helena had seen enough. She never would have used any kind of drugs. And she wouldn't have stood by while Rupert did, either. She must not have known until it was too late."

But when Helena found his body on that fateful night, she must have known right away that he had been using again, that he had sniffed himself high and then fallen into the pool to his death.

We don't dwell on the source of my mother's terror, on all that must have gone through her thoughts as she considered what to do next, but the struggle is vivid in my mind as I know it must be in theirs. The authorities would surely have exonerated her of any guilt. But what about her father-in-law, what of his many threats, now that Rupert was no longer there to protect her? What could she do, young, alone, newly married and away from everything she knew, with such a threat bearing down on her?

And so, most likely spurred by blind panic, Helena ran, stopping only to grab her backpack and throw in some essentials.

Which was her own undoing.

"I flew to Kuala Lumpur to collect her things," Nana says. "They'd bought matching backpacks for the trip. She told me about them in her letter before she left. His was never found. But hers was still lying there in the hotel room."

His backpack on her back. His pack with the secret compartment stuffed with his newly acquired bags of white powder, feeding a habit that had claimed one life and was about to swallow up another. The drugs were found by the Thai border patrol, and Helena Finn was quickly locked away—so quickly, in fact, that the alert had not yet gone out placing her as a person of interest in the case of her dead husband. By the time the call did go out, Helena had slid into the depths of the Thai prison system, from which she would not come out alive.

"She could have done something to help herself," I say,

mostly for my own ears. "Anytime she wanted, she could have. At least she could have tried. But she was too afraid. She chose to bury herself in her secrets. It was the only way she knew to fight back."

I close my eyes while the buzz of conversation continues around me. In my mind I see Mama as she was, filling our cell like a sunburst—so desperate for life that she chose fear, yet too bound by her fear to really live. Did she never wonder if things had to be that way, if there might have been another path? What if she *had* gone back, had faced old Payne down? Which one of them would have broken first?

And then I remember Mama's final moments, her last words to me. With a rush of realization, the blinds fall away from my mind. All that talk of secrets and promises . . . and how little I'd understood! In those last, dying moments, I now realize, Mama finally saw the truth. In the end, she saw her secrets for what they really were: not cloaks but chains.

Don't, she tried to tell me. *Don't do what I did. Don't be held in by secrets. Break free.*

And I did, Mama, I tell her. Even without understanding what you were saying, I did. Your message came through in the end.

You didn't know it, but you were winning the battle all along.

And now, so have I.

47

Almost a full day has passed since Payne burst in on us, and I am growing more accustomed to his blustery, egocentric ways. He's a bit like a spoiled child who expects everyone to do everything he says, but deep down is afraid that nobody loves who he truly is.

With good reason.

Still, in spite of all I know about him, in spite of all he has done, I am finding it harder and harder to dislike him. It's obvious now that his breakdown in my room was less the thing of a moment and more the accumulated weight of years of shame and guilt. He now seems curiously eager to start over, to be a different sort of tyrant than the one he's been. He'll always rule, of course. That's the way he is. Nana and I scurry around, bringing him Scotch and water, fetching the newspaper, and rolling our eyes at each other behind his back. But for all his gruff manner, he is family. And I have little enough of that left.

Both he and Nana rented rooms for the night, and it's now evening, my fourth day in America, and we are walking along the coast and looking out over the bay. It's a special day, Nana has told me, a day when the whole country celebrates a long-ago victory of independence. I decide that this day should hold my own celebration, too. There's something I've wanted to do for a long time.

While Payne sits on a nearby bench, watching with hawk's eyes, I move along the shore, looking for just the right things. Loy Krathong, the Festival of Light, is not until November, but I can't wait that long. There's a full moon rising out over the water, and everything about the night, the air, the soft summer breeze, feels right.

I find just what I'm looking for: a wide, round piece of bark that is firm and curves up a bit at the edges. It's about the size of a saucer—a little small, but it will do. Nana stands next to me, watching as I assemble my *krathong*. Then she takes a few steps back, joining Payne in observing me from a distance. Perhaps she can tell how much I need to be alone right now. On my own, to do this one last thing.

My raft will be simple, compared to the ones I've seen back home. Isra loved to take me out for this festival—the lights floating down the river, mixed with the glowing lanterns drifting up into the night sky, are some of my favorite memories. It's so far away, that old life, yet it's also a part of me that will never fully disappear. And that's what has brought me out tonight, to honor my past and show gratitude for my journey.

Working carefully, I cover the base of my *krathong* in soft green leaves. To this I add some flowers I've been able to find—wiry yellow ones and small soft blue ones, and a few that are a bold pink. I arrange them in a pattern, with the pink ones clustered together in the middle. Once it looks beautiful, I add my mementos: the last of the *baht* that Isra gave me and the scrap of paper with Mama's listing of names and addresses in Bangkok. On top of this I place my square of embroidered cloth, the piece I began with Yai but never finished. I touch it carefully, stroking the clumsy green and brown stitches. There's still no image there that I can see. But it feels right to let it go like this.

That's what Loy Krathong is about, after all—letting go. It's a time to loosen hold of the past and to look toward the future. It's a time to begin life afresh, to look at the world through brand-new eyes. And it's a time to remember the dead, to honor those who have gone before.

"This is for you, Mama," I whisper.

I don't know where the road ahead will take me, this new life I am just beginning to taste. Behind me, Payne is bickering with Nana about where I will live. They are so different, these two, yet curiously alike. For a second I picture myself following Payne into his fancy limousine with the dark tinted windows, pulling up to his palatial mansion, and flying in his private helicopter wherever the fancy strikes me. Then I picture myself holding Nana's hand as I cross the same threshold my mother passed over so many times, as I make her house my home, as I learn about her from the beginning forward. Those are just two of the forks my road has ahead; I know there will be many more to come.

And then I know that it doesn't matter what road I take. My life's no fairy tale, and it's taken long enough to get me this far, but somehow I know that whatever's up ahead, I've found my happily ever after.

I'm wearing it on the inside, and nothing can ever change that.

I reach into my pocket and pull out the matchbook I brought from the hotel. I should have candles to do this properly, but it doesn't matter. Moving quickly, I strike match after match, crisscrossing them into a burning heap in the center of my raft. The little boat bobs in the shallows and once it starts to blaze I give it a gentle push and it floats out toward the bay.

In the sky overhead, fireworks explode—my new country celebrating this day of my rebirth. I look down at the flaming embroidery at the top of my pile as it moves away from me—and suddenly I see it. There *is* a picture there. The green and brown thread is starting to sizzle and crackle but for a second I see it clear as day: a tree.

But not a bare, dark, stunted tree like the one I drew strength from when I was on the inside.

This tree is heavy with leaves and bursting with life. It is tall and straight and proud. A tree like that, I think, could take the storms and still stand. It could hold its ground no matter what the world threw at it.

I have crossed the world for this moment, for this feeling of looking out at the world, knowing it is there for my taking. I have slipped through the bars and they didn't bite. They couldn't hold me. The wind calls my name.

My raft sails farther out toward the sea, now a sputtering ball of flames. It doesn't matter. The image of that tree will be with me always. It's inside me now.

This tree will live forever.

ACKNOWLEDGMENTS

So many people have had a part in helping to bring this book to life: to each and every one of you—and to the many others I haven't named here—I give my heartfelt thanks and appreciation.

Firstly, to my stellar editor, Stacy Cantor Abrams, who saw the potential in my early draft and helped me make it all that it could be; and to Erin Murphy, who is all things wonderful and magnificent, pretty much a dream come true.

To my critique group and writing partners, who read countless versions, pulled me out of holes, brainstormed with me, and provided encouragement, input, and listening ears galore: Natalie Lorenzi, Cynthia Omololu, Julie Phillips, and Kip Wilson; Kate Messner; Nancy Viau; John Bell, Mordena Babich, Karen Day, Kathryn Hulick, Ed Loechler, Mitali Perkins, Laya Steinberg, and Tui Sutherland.

To all my fabulous clients and the rest of the Gango: you guys are the best. Literally.

To the NESCBWI for awarding this manuscript the 2009 Ruth Landers Glass Scholarship, for helping me believe there just might be something to this story of a girl with a most unusual name.

To Euan Harvey, Brianne and Brooke Bryant, and Elli Wollard, who scrutinized my Thai language and culture references and helped me correct my many errors. Any remaining missteps are entirely my own. To the representatives from the Port of Oakland, for answering my string of random questions, and to my uncle John, for providing essential input on immigration by ship.

And lastly—but of crowning importance—to Zack, Kimberly, and Lauren. I'm so blessed to have you in my life. I can't think of anything better than this moment, me and you and all of us. Gratitude doesn't even come close.